Second Helpings a

A quirky romantic novella about a reformed ex-con and the enterprising young woman who helps him rediscover his self-worth... Jacobs creates an enchanting world. A charming story for those who enjoy a quick, action-packed, romantic fairy tale.

—Kirkus

With *Second Helpings at the Serve You Right Café*, her follow-up to her wildly satisfying debut novel, *Wrong Place, Wrong Time*, Tilia Klebenov Jacobs proves her success is no fluke. Jacobs, who teaches writing to prison inmates, has used her experience and insight to craft a highly entertaining yet deeply moving story about an ex-con trying to make a fresh start while facing an enemy who doesn't want him to go straight. The café itself is as real as any location in fiction, a place so vividly rendered you can smell the coffee and taste the scones, and its patrons create a tapestry of the town of Oxbridge, in Western Massachusetts, where the novel is set. The characterizations are rich and detailed, full of charm as well as complexity. Emet and Mercey are star-crossed lovers the reader desperately wants to have a chance. For that to happen, Emet has to free himself from the past, and the stigma and suspicion that come with it. *Second Helpings* is the story of his struggle to do so, and the reader is with him every step of the way, hanging on his every decision, suffering his every setback, holding out hope that Emet—like all of us, really—will get the second chance he deserves.

—Peter Ullian, award-winning and critically acclaimed author of *Big Bossman* and *The Triumphant Return of Blackbird Flynt*.

The Serve You Right Café is a place where readers will enjoy getting a taste of unexpected romance and a dash of suspense.... The themes of the story paint a portrait of redemption and, like its title, the rare beauty of second chances.

—IndieReader.com

Tilia Jacobs' gripping novella, *Second Helpings*, is a witty, heartwarming story about finding redemption and love in all the right places. Vivid prose, brilliant dialogue, and elegant description add sparkle and punch to this fresh, masterfully told story. But it's the generous spirit, nuanced insight, and riveting cast of characters that capture the reader's heart and make *Second Helpings* such a brilliant, unforgettable read.

—Terri Giuliano Long, author of *In Leah's Wake*

Tilia Klebenov Jacobs writes with a deep heart and sparkling wit about second chances and the power of friendship. Her novel has it all: characters you'll love spending time with; crackling, pitch-perfect dialog; and a plot that builds to a powerful conclusion. A winning story from a writer to watch!

—Elisabeth Elo, author of *North of Boston*

Also by Tilia Klebenov Jacobs

Wrong Place, Wrong Time

Second Helpings at the Serve You Right Café

Tilia Klebenov Jacobs

First published 2015 in the United States of America by
Linden Tree Press

First edition

ISBN: 978-0-9898601-6-1 (Linden Tree Press)

This is a work of fiction. Names, characters, places, and events appear as the result of the imagination of the author. Any resemblance to real persons living or dead, places, or events is a matter of coincidence.

To my family.

You know who you are.

To Sharon —
Help yourself!
– [illegible]

Second Helpings

at the

Serve You Right Café

Friday, September 19

Hours of Operation:

6:00 am to 7:00 pm

1

Emet's dark eyes sparked. "I did it," he said. "I asked her out."

"She said yes?" said Eden Rose.

"She did."

Eden Rose held up her hand for a high five. Emet slapped it. As if their hands had chimed, a dinger went off. Emet turned to an oven set in the brick wall and removed a tray of scones, thick and triangular and lightly browned.

"On the counter," said Eden Rose.

"Flavor icing?"

"Cardamom-cinnamon. In the fridge. But wait—"

"—till they cool," he finished, setting them down.

Eden smiled. Her mouth was usually about to smile. She walked past the glass-topped pastry counter that separated the kitchen from the customer area, and took down chairs that had spent the night with their feet in the air. Predawn darkness still painted the windows from the outside, and Eden flipped a series of switches, making the inside glow but saving the sidewalk illumination until she and Emet opened the Serve You Right Café.

Emet opened the stainless-steel fridge and pulled out a white canister marked "C^2 Icing," followed by the previous day's date on a strip of masking tape. He pulled off the lid and stirred the stiff mixture with a wooden spoon till it softened, falling in ribbons flecked with burgundy specks.

Emet was in his early thirties, and had been working for Eden Rose for a month. His last name was First, which had confused his teachers back when he was in school. Emet was not tall, but he looked tall, probably because his cheekbones were high and his frame was lanky. His hair, which was held back with a net, was soft and shaggy and so black it was almost blue. Emet's eyes were dark and his smile was bright. He was part Native American, and he called himself Eden's Sioux chef.

Eden Rose finished turning on the lights, but kept the shades drawn. She and Emet had an hour before the morning caffeine junkies lurched in the door. After that would come the college students and novelists with Dells and Macs. Many of them stayed all day, or most of it, which was fine: customers walking by on the street would come into a crowded eatery and stand in line for unknown pastries and drinks, but they mistrusted an empty establishment.

In mid-afternoon the moms would come with toddlers in tow and babies in slings and strollers. The moms loved the Serve You Right Café because much of the food was organic and also because Eden Rose had put an armchair in a nook and curtained it off for discreet breastfeeding. Sometimes the toddlers went with their mothers; other times they stayed in the restaurant area and drew knee-high pictures on the chalkboard that covered half of one wall.

After the moms and kids left, things got quieter. A neighborhood cop would come in several times a week for coffee. He always paid, but Eden Rose gave him free refills. Then he and perhaps his partner would leave and the last poet would pack up her computer and put away her Moleskine notebook and the door would shut and Eden and Emet would dismantle the day, sweeping crumbs off the floor, wiping down the tables, and putting up the chairs.

"When's the date?" said Eden.

"Tonight. After work."

"So," said Eden Rose, "have you told her…?"

"No," said Emet. He was filling an icing bag with the grey mixture, squeezing it gently to work out the air pockets. "Not yet."

"Going to?"

"I'll tell her," said Emet. "I just don't know when."

Eden Rose set down the last of the chairs. She helped Emet fill the display case with the day's bounty: scones and muffins and croissants (plain, chocolate, spinach and cheese); whole bananas, cut cantaloupe in glowing orange cubes, and strawberries with yogurt and granola; and juice and milk in boxes with straws glued to the sides in plastic sleeves. Emet filled the whipped cream canisters and Eden loaded the coffee machines. She put fresh flowers in bottles and vases that hung on the walls in the darker corners, because they seemed to make the shadows brighter.

Nothing at the Serve You Right Café was new, but all of it was solid. Some of the tables had round tops of dark wood that had been varnished a quarter of an inch thick. Others were square, with checkerboards built in. Eden counted out the right number of red and black pieces and put them in heavy glasses at the counter. The regulars all knew to ask. The cash register had buttons instead of a touch screen. Taped to its front was a check in a plastic bag. A note card above it read, "I'm sure your check is good, but his wasn't. Cash or credit only, please." The check was stamped "Insufficient Funds" in red across its face.

"Hard to know the right time to bring it up," said Eden Rose.

Emet nodded. "Pretty much sucks the air out of the room,"

Eden Rose picked a piece of chalk out of a tin cup bolted to the wall next to the blackboard. Standing on a chair and reaching as high as she could get while still making the letters pretty, she wrote, "SIX-WORD MEMOIR." She climbed down, put away the chalk, wiped off the chair, and put it back at its table.

"Well," she said, "there may not be a right time to talk about it. But when you do, you'll know a lot about her."

Emet sighed and smiled at the same time. "And she'll know a lot about me."

Eden Rose flipped the Closed sign and unlocked the door. Groggy commuters lined up at the counter, where the air already tasted like coffee. "You ought to put in a drive-through," grumbled one man, tapping the edge of his credit card against the counter as Emet assembled his order.

"The city won't let us," said Eden Rose. Her voice was bright as cherries. "Besides, if we did that I wouldn't get to see you, Gary."

Gary snorted. "Reason number one to bribe a city councilor, right there." Emet, adding the last pouf of whipped cream to Gary's travel mug, flashed a smile at the coffee before handing it over. Gary grunted, dropped a generous tip in the jar, and left.

A woman in a business suit ordered a nonfat mocha and told Eden Rose how tangled her toddler's hair got when she washed it, and how the little girl cried. Eden, who had no children, recommended a light, leave-in conditioner. The woman took her drink and left. A college student with flat hair and a goatee told Eden that his mother was doing much better. Eden gave him a smile and a banana-chip muffin to celebrate. People put away their Blackberries and iGadgets to place their orders and talk to Eden, and the line moved steadily.

People told Eden Rose all sorts of things without knowing why. It was not her looks, which were pleasant but ordinary. She was in that generic age between thirty and forty-nine, on the tall side of short, and well-groomed with carob-colored hair held back in a ponytail. The urge to confide in her, which few resisted, probably had something to do with her eyes. People tended to find themselves there. Eden's eyes were a clear brown that made drunks think of smooth whiskey and nature lovers remember woodland pools. Southerners looked into her eyes and tasted the memory of sweet tea, and a homeless man saw the darkness of a safe place to sleep.

"Got a few," said Emet, gesturing at the blackboard with his chin because his hands were full. Under SIX-WORD MEMOIR were several lines in different handwritings.

We fight. He wins. I cry.

I don't want to be friends.

How do I know it's mine?

"Somebody had a bad week," said Emet.

"They've been up all night," said Eden Rose. Excluding commuters, the morning crowd was often heavily weighted toward insomniacs and broken-hearted lovers. The former glugged coffee as though enough of it would save their lives; the latter ordered food which they shredded with their forks but did not eat. "Sun's barely up. Give them a little more time."

Half an hour later, more lines had appeared.

Slave to caffeine. Love my master.

OMG! Only six words?

"That one's pretty good," said Emet. There was a lull in the flow of customers, and he wiped his hands on the towel that hung from the string of his apron before pointing.

For sale: baby shoes, never worn.

"Very good," agreed Eden Rose.

"I hope it's not true."

"It's not."

"How do you know?"

"Because it's Hemingway." She raised her voice. "Hey, Andy. Plagiarists pay double in this establishment."

A twenty-year-old in a black tee shirt gave an abashed, got-me grin. He wiped the words away and picked up a stick of chalk. After a pause he wrote a new line and sat down again.

Can't do it. Got writer's block.

"Better," said Eden Rose. Andy smiled again and ducked behind a massive anthology entitled *Grandeur and Despair: Twentieth-Century American Writers*.

Eden Rose fetched a tray of blueberry muffins from the back room where they had been cooling. Her sleeves were rolled up, and her biceps were laddered with short, white burn scars. The scent of baking mixed with the russet aroma of kukicha as Emet scooped it into a tea ball and set it to steep in a sunshine-yellow teapot for a customer. Keyboards clicked in a counterpoint of fits and starts, and a businessman lunged for his phone as it rang with the opening bars of "Born to Run."

The café was full of sideways afternoon light by the time Marty the cop walked in. Emet excused himself for an overdue break while Eden got Marty's regular order. The light made her fingers the color of honey, and she chatted easily with him about people they knew. Marty left, and a few minutes later Emet returned. He put his apron back on and wiped down the counter.

"You know everyone around here," he said.

"I run a coffee shop."

"Yeah, but it's more than that. Any time I see you outside work, someone's saying hi or telling you their life story."

Eden's chin dipped like an ice cube plunking into a drink. "That's because of AA."

Emet raised an eyebrow and glanced at the door. "Marty?"

Eden smiled enigmatically. "The second A is for Anonymous."

Emet finished wiping the counter and tossed the cloth in a hamper before slipping a new one onto the front of his apron. "Sorry. Didn't mean to pry."

"That's okay."

"I knew a lot of guys in AA," he said. "It's a good program."

Eden Rose smiled again. "You?"

"No," he said. "That was never my problem."

"It was surely mine," she said. "Except for a long time I thought it wasn't, because I only drank wine."

Emet's face lit up. "That's what one of the guys told me. He thought he wasn't an addict because he only smoked dope on weekends, and he thought he wasn't an alcoholic because he only drank beer on weeknights."

Eden laughed out loud. "More than a river in Egypt."

"What? Oh—right."

The big, central room was empty, the chairs askew. Emet looked at the light illuminating the chalkboard, which was so full that the newest entries had to climb vertically up the margins.

Adventure calls with its klaxon cry.

Wish I were anywhere but here.

Don't die not knowing. Bungee jump!

"That's not how I feel," he said.

"It's not?"

Emet barely shook his head. "All I want to do is live an honorable, old-fashioned life. I want simple things. I don't mind working for them. But I've had enough thrills to last me."

He did not look at her. The room was not silent, because the refrigerator hummed, and they still had jazz playing low; and outside, the wind soughed in the trees. But it felt silent, and the silence felt heavy.

"What was it like for you," said Eden Rose, "when you got out?"

He drew a breath and let it out in little puffs, as if he did not want to laugh. “Like the air was made of color and I could breathe for the first time.”

There was another pause. Norah Jones came on the speaker and sang that she didn’t know why she hadn’t come. Eden Rose opened her hands. “I can’t imagine.”

“No,” he agreed. “I don’t suppose you can.” He turned to look at her, and gave a half-smile that glinted in the late light. “Then again, I was never an alcoholic.”

“I still am an alcoholic.”

“I guess we all have stories to tell,” said Emet.

Eden glanced at her watch. “Could you close up? I have to take some stuff across the street.”

“Sure thing.”

Eden grabbed a paper bag from the counter. At the door she paused. “When’s your date?” she said.

“I have time. She works late.”

“Well,” she said, “enjoy.”

“I’ll do my best.”

Eden Rose walked across the street, paper bag in hand, and sat on a certain park bench. Overhead the streetlights came on as daylight crumbled into dusk. Behind the old mill buildings that were now condos and computer stores, the spires of Worthington College glowed in the last of the light. Up and down the street, doors opened and people came out carrying garbage bags which they pumped into plastic cans. They tamped down the lids and dragged the cans to the curb, scraping them on the sidewalk before going back inside. Some came back and set out bins for recycling. A woman walked by with a pug who grinned, pop-eyed, at the dusk, his legs flashing in a stiff-kneed trot. A plastic bag hung from the woman's free hand. She dropped it into one of the trash cans and kept walking.

The park took up more than a city block, having been built over the terminus of the railroad after the last of Oxbridge's ancient pines had rumbled out of town on flatbed cars almost a hundred years earlier. It was guarded around the perimeter by a procession of sycamores and willows, under which ran a paved walkway. At one end was a playground, with slides and wooden structures hung with loops and rope ladders and nets for climbing. In front of Eden Rose was a plaza containing stone benches and a multi-tiered fountain whose ragged domes of water looked like an inverted chandelier. Eden Rose waited.

Presently an elderly couple walked around the fountain, arm-in-arm. He was dressed in a baggy tuxedo, she in a beaded flapper dress that shimmered like water when she walked. They looked like a tall, dark tree with a solitary bloom at its side. Eden Rose stood up.

"Isadore," she said. "Daisy. How nice of you to come."

"Isn't it a lovely evening?" said the woman. "And you're looking just as sweet as ever."

"Sit, please," urged the man. Eden sat, and the couple arranged themselves on the bench.

Eden picked up the bag. "Ready for a little market research?"

"As ever," said Isadore, and Eden handed over the bag. While they removed a scone and a thick slice of dark bread with pumpkin seeds on its crust, she pulled a notebook out of her pocket and flipped it open.

"I think you have the açai berry scone and the flaxseed pumpkin bread," she said.

"That's the hot new thing, isn't it?" said Daisy, looking at Isadore's scone. "Açai berry."

"Full of antioxidants but low in sugar," said Eden Rose. "Emet's worried about the flavor balance."

Isadore took a bite and chewed thoughtfully. He swallowed. "Honestly, it's a little bland. You might want to sweeten it a bit more, maybe add some icing. Hope you don't mind my saying that."

"Of course not," said Eden. She bent over her notebook and jotted a few words. "This is very helpful. Okay, Daisy, your turn."

Isadore finished his scone while Daisy sampled her bread and told Eden that it was surprisingly "substantial," and that the pumpkin seeds were a nice touch. Eden took copious notes while the couple reached into the bag and pulled out an oatmeal muffin and a croissant stuffed with rainbow chard and goat cheese. These, too, were sacrificed in the name of research while the three discussed the relative merits of lemon extract versus zest, and the necessity of having eggs at room temperature before beating.

"Hey," said a voice behind Eden Rose. She turned. "I got the sourdough started," said Emet. "It's by the pilot light."

"Thanks." She slid on her bench. "Care to join us?"

Emet sat. "Evening, Isadore, Daisy."

"Hi, Emet," said Daisy. Isadore nodded, his mouth full.

"So how's the magic business?"

Isadore swallowed. "Enchanting." He took a coin out of his pocket and made it flip along his knuckles before it disappeared. He opened his hand, which was of course empty. "Never gets old."

"And neither do we," chimed in Daisy. She leaned against her husband, smiling up at him. "Isn't that right?"

When Isadore smiled, his brows lowered slightly. They were dark and shaggy and looked like feral hedgerows. His neatly combed hair was shot with grey. Daisy's face, glowing in the light from the streetlamp, was a bouquet of wrinkles. "Not so far as I can tell," he said.

Daisy snuggled closer to Isadore and peered around him to see Emet. "How's the baking business?" she said.

"Making lots of dough," said Emet brightly. Daisy burst into giggles.

"Stop making time with my girl," said Isadore. "Meet you at dawn with pistols, laddie."

"Guess I better watch myself," said Emet. "Daisy, it's no good. I've found someone else."

She pushed herself upright. "Have you really?"

"Um." Emet smiled at the fountain. "Maybe. I don't know yet."

"What do you mean, you don't know yet?" barked Isadore. "Good heavens, man, do you love this girl or don't you? Take her in your arms. Declare yourself!"

"The ladies love that," said Daisy.

"Absolutely," said Eden Rose. "Especially on a first date."

"Oh, it's a first date?" said Isadore. "Well, that's different. You might want to take your time a bit in that case."

"That was kind of the plan," said Emet.

"This is your first date in—some time, isn't it, dear?" said Daisy.

"Nine and a half years," said Emet. "A little more."

A smile blossomed on Daisy's face, and her green eyes sparkled like the water in the fountain. "Oh, my. It really *is* a first date, isn't it? I'm so happy for you, dear heart. Even though of course I'm utterly broken-hearted for myself," she added, snuggling back against Isadore.

Isadore's arm went around Daisy like a vine. "So who's the young lady?"

"She's a physical therapist," said Emet. "I'm seeing her tonight after her shift."

"How did you meet her?"

"In line at a doughnut shop on the way to work. She, um, didn't have her wallet so I paid for her Danish." A shadow dusted his cheeks.

Now it was Eden's turn to be outraged. "A *doughnut shop?* On your way to work at *my café?"*

"It just happened," protested Emet. "It meant nothing to me, I swear."

"Tell it to the scones," said Eden. "They're the ones you've really betrayed."

"Still, paying for her breakfast, that's good," said Isadore. "Helping a damsel in distress. Well played, Emet First, well played."

"Oh, hush, you old goof," said Daisy. "Emet, dear, as your most recent girlfriend—and just remember, *I* broke up with *you*—I feel I have a right to ask. Does this young lady know why you've gone so long between dates?"

Emet rubbed the fingers of one hand across the knuckles of the other. "Not yet."

"Don't worry, dearest," said Daisy. "Once she sees what a lovely person you are, nothing else will matter."

"I don't agree," said Isadore. He straightened, pulling his arm away from Daisy. "This is a tricky business, young fellow. If you tell her too early, it's the only thing she knows about you and she might decide you're not worth the trouble. Tell her too late and it'll look like you were hiding something. Now she thinks you're a liar. Next thing you know, some gallant young swain has stolen her away from you."

"If I'm lucky, there's no gallant swain," said Emet.

"Oh, son." Isadore's face was serious, and it looked as deeply lined as driftwood. "There's always a gallant swain."

Daisy slapped him lightly on the chest. "Not everyone is the Amazing Isadore, you know."

"What do you mean?" said Eden Rose.

Daisy smiled with a naughty secret. "I was engaged before I married Isadore."

"Were you really?" said Eden Rose.

"Oh, yes."

"He was a cad," said Isadore.

"I'm sure they don't want to hear about this, dear heart," said Daisy.

"I do," said Emet. "What happened?"

Eden Rose said nothing, but folded her hands and leaned forward with an exaggerated air of expectation. Daisy spread her hands before her in mock protest.

"Honestly, you two. All right, then, but I'll say this for him: if he was a cad, he wasn't very good at it. Actually, he was a nice boy—I thought—and from a good family. College educated, and all set to go into his father's business. His family liked me and my family liked him. I would have been very comfortable, you know."

"But you didn't really love him," said Emet.

"That's where you're wrong, dear. I loved him very deeply, and I think he loved me."

"So what happened?" said Emet.

"One night he told me he couldn't take me to a dance because he was visiting a sick friend. But after he left, the friend called me from the dance to ask why I wasn't there."

"Oops," said Eden Rose.

"Oops indeed. So I figured out where he was—don't ask me how—and went over there. He was playing poker with his frat fellows. And losing." Her mouth tightened in disgust.

The fountain splashed, and overhead the leaves hissed in a light breeze. Emet broke the silence. "So you broke up with him?"

"On the spot, dearie. And my mother was *outraged.*"

"With him."

"With me, dear. For breaking it off. And his father called to talk to my father, and *they* wanted me to go back to him. And his mother started stalking me at synagogue—not that she'd ever gone before then, even though she was a member—trying to patch things up. And oh my gracious, the gifts and promises from the boy himself! Of course I sent them all back."

"So what was it?" said Emet. "The gambling or the losing?"

"Neither."

Emet blinked. "Neither?"

"Anyone can have a bad night at cards," said Daisy. "And I played poker myself, back then. I probably could have cleaned his clock."

Isadore pulled a packet of cards from his pocket and fanned them out.

"So…." Emet groped. "The dance?"

"The lie," said Daisy. "I just decided, if he would lie about playing cards with his friends, what else was he going to lie about? There were plenty of dances. I would have understood if he'd just said he didn't want to go. But he thought I was a silly bit of fluff who wasn't worth telling the truth to. Life's too short for that."

"Worked out okay for me," said Isadore smugly. He snapped the cards shut, and flicked out the Queen of Hearts, which he presented to Daisy with a half-bow. "We were married six months later."

Daisy took the card and pressed it to her chest in mock passion. "Fifty years ago. And I never looked back."

"Forty-nine," said Isadore.

"Fifty this year, my gallant swain."

"What did your family think?" said Eden Rose.

"When I took up with a street magician?" Daisy's laugh bloomed in the night. "There was a period of adjustment, dear."

"What about the other boy?" said Eden Rose. "Did you ever see him again?"

"Not after he gave up weeping under my bedroom window, no. Crocodile tears," she said to Emet. "Don't feel sorry for him. When I married Isadore, my ex's family decided I had gone off my rocker, and they were ecstatic. I'm sure they told him he'd dodged a crazy-lady bullet and was better off without me."

"We almost used Crazy-Lady Bullet for her stage name," said Isadore. He put a coin in his hand, shut his fingers over it, and opened it to reveal a bouquet of multicolored tissue paper flowers. "But my manager at the time thought Lovely Assistant would pull in a more respectable crowd." He handed her the bouquet.

"Oh, Isadore, what am I supposed to do with all this?" she scolded. "You know this dress doesn't have pockets."

"So what's your secret?" said Emet. "Never say you're visiting a sick friend when the guy's actually at a dance?"

"That's part of it, I guess," said Isadore. "I'm a magician. I mislead people all the time. But I never lie."

Emet and Eden Rose watched The Amazing Isadore and his Lovely Assistant walk into the dusk on the other side of the fountain.

"What did they have for dinner tonight?" he said.

"Açai berry scone, filled croissants, and a few other things."

Emet twisted to look at her. "What did they think of the açai berry?"

"Isadore thought it was a little bland."

"Would he go sweeter or more tart?"

"He said sweeter."

"I'll try it both ways," said Emet. "See if I have time tomorrow."

"They'll be happy to test the beta version."

"Where do they live?"

"Somewhere in the park," said Eden.

Emet sat upright. "What, like in a box or something?"

"I don't know. I've never followed them."

"Are they going to be okay?"

“I think so,” said Eden Rose. “There’s no frost in the forecast, and their daughter keeps an eye on them.”

“They stay with her when it gets cold?”

Eden Rose shook her head. “She calls Marty and has them arrested for vagrancy.”

“No way.”

“So they don’t die of exposure. The county jail’s right here in Oxbridge, and they like it more than the homeless shelter. Everyone knows them, and they say the food’s better.”

Emet smiled humorlessly. “Three hots and a cot.”

“What?”

“I knew guys that every fall would commit some kind of offense so they’d be on the inside come the snow,” said Emet. “That’s what they called it.”

“Really?”

“They loved it. Get to hang with their buddies all winter, score drugs, have sex.”

“And they didn’t have any other way of getting by?”

“They didn’t think so.”

“That’s so sad.”

“No, it’s not,” said Emet. “I don’t grieve much for some guy who beats up his girlfriend just so he won’t have to pay rent.”

“These,” said Eden Rose, “are two very different situations.”

"True."

"Daisy and Isadore think the world of Marty."

"He called after you left," said Emet.

"Marty did?"

"Yeah. You're not the only person to get ripped off lately."

"Oh?"

"The guy's been writing rubber checks all over town, usually for under twenty dollars so no one asks for ID. Or else he says he forgot it."

"That's what he did with me," said Eden Rose. "Felt in his pockets and everything. I'd already put the order together, so I said I'd take a check. He thanked me about five times."

"The checkbook was stolen," said Emet. "The owner closed the account."

Eden sighed. "Thanks for not saying anything in front of Daisy and Isadore."

"If I had a middle name," said Emet, "it would be Discretion with a capital D."

"How else would you spell Discretion if it were your middle name?"

Emet chuckled, but Eden Rose sighed and shook her head. "The return fees cost more than the meal," she said.

"Jerk."

"I hate criminals." She glanced at him. "No offense."

"None taken." A smile lit Emet's voice, and he leaned back on the park bench. "You know, the whole time I was in there, the nicest thing that happened to me was when one of the COs told me I wasn't a criminal."

"And a CO is…."

"Corrections Officer. Guard," he translated.

"What did he mean?"

"He said, 'You're not a criminal. Even though you're in here, you're no criminal.'" He smiled again. "Honest to God, I glowed from that for days. I bet it sounds small, but it wasn't."

"It sounds like it was pretty big at the time," said Eden Rose.

"Huge."

They listened to the sounds of the park: night insects and a distant conversation that carried through the evening air, and behind it all the plash-plash of the fountain.

"What was the worst thing?" said Eden Rose.

"While I was on the inside, you mean?"

"Yes."

"You really want to know?"

"Kind of," she said.

Emet looked at a place that was distant and bleak. "I saw two of my buddies die." He waited, and when Eden Rose said nothing he went on. "We were in the rec yard and some of the guys wanted to play handball. I'm like, sure, I'll get the ball. So I went and got it and I'm headed back to the yard. And then there's all this running, and a voice over the PA goes, *'Freeze it up! Freeze it up!'*"

"And that means…."

"It means wherever you are, you freeze. No movement. And the PA's blaring so loud it shakes your lungs. Then the CO on my unit yells, *'Lock in.'* Everyone goes into their cells, fast. The doors slam shut—"

"All at the same time?"

Emet nodded. "There's a guy in a gallery, like a booth, and he controls everything from inside. It's black glass, so he sees the whole unit but you can't see him. So now everyone's locked down and no one knows why, but we can hear radio chatter and the COs are all running to battle stations. Then I hear screaming outside. My cell had a window over the yard, so I saw it. There was an outdoor weightlifting area, and bunch of gangbangers had smuggled the weights under their shirts. They were smashing the other guys with them, just breaking in their heads. And I saw my roommate go down, and a guy I worked with. Then the COs are all over everyone, and a bunch more guys go down." Emet's voice was steady; the story was worn smooth and dark by retelling. "They brought them in—there was blood everywhere. And I had to clean it up. Me and some other guys. I had a mop and a bucket, and by the end of it the water in the pail was the color of ketchup." He stared at the fountain. "That's what I was doing before I started baking açai berry scones."

"God," said Eden Rose.

"Don't pity me," said Emet. "I was there, I survived, and now I'm out."

"I didn't say I pitied you."

Emet turned to her. "Why did you hire me?"

"You were qualified."

Emet was a graduate of a prison culinary arts program. His classmates had included junkies, drug dealers, a wide range of murderers, and a Harvard MBA who had lived a life of glittering excess until the audit.

Where food was concerned, Emet had magic in his fingers. He kept his knives laser sharp and twice as bright. He could cut strawberries so they looked like roses, and wrap up leftovers in aluminum foil twisted into the shape of a swan. Emet made marshmallow caterpillars that humped over the tops of cupcakes, and his madeleines tasted like the breath of spring flowers. When Emet looked at ingredients, he saw the palate of a rainbow.

"A lot of guys are qualified," he said. "Most aren't ex-cons."

"I figured you probably deserved a second chance," said Eden. Her brown eyes were clear.

"Why?"

"What makes you so curious?" she said.

His shoulders shifted. "I don't know how people see me."

"Oh," she said. "Well, I didn't know if you deserved a second chance or not. But if you didn't, then probably I didn't either. And I don't know if I deserved it, but I got one, once, a long time ago. So I was willing to take the risk."

"Oh," said Emet. "Well…thanks."

"You're welcome."

"Second chance?" he said.

"Yes."

"Should I ask?"

"There's a reason I'm in AA," she said.

Emet stared into the darkness. "Hell," he said finally. "How am I going to tell her the best thing that happened to me in nine and a half years was someone telling me I wasn't a criminal?"

Eden Rose wadded up the paper bag and tossed it into a garbage can. “Daisy’s right,” she said. “This woman could just plain old like you. It happens.”

“Maybe.” Emet sounded unconvinced.

“You have a job and a place of your own,” said Eden Rose. “You’re not doing too badly.”

“My own place, my own job, and my very own parole officer.”

“You’re not the only person who ever did time,” she chided him. “The Apostle Paul wrote part of the New Testament when he was in prison in Rome. And Martin Luther King was in jail in Birmingham.”

“Martin Luther King didn’t pull nine and a half years,” said Emet. “And Paul wasn’t big into dating, if I remember my Bible correctly.”

“Come to think of it, Paul actually died in prison.”

“Guess I’m one up on him, then.”

“That’s the spirit.”

Emet glanced at his watch. "She's off in an hour. Maybe by that time I'll have stopped feeling sorry for myself."

Eden stood up. "Emet, I hate to say this, but relax. I know it feels like you have a lot riding on this, but really you don't. She already knows you a little, and she likes you well enough to get together after work. Ask her about her job and her favorite movies. Talk about the weather. If it doesn't work out, so what? Everybody has dating horror stories. You can always try again. And you've been through a lot worse than a bad date."

Emet smiled at her. "Do you ever get tired of being right?"

"Never. It's a constant thrill."

He stood. "I'm going home. Walk you to your place?"

She shook her head. "I need to go through the receipts. I'll be fine," she said as his mouth opened. "Marty comes through a couple of times a night. And I'll be done in half an hour anyway. Go home and wash the flour out of your hair."

"Do I have flour in my hair?"

"You do."

"Guess I better go home and wash it out."

Emet walked away on the pathway under the willows and sycamores, and Eden Rose crossed the street and unlocked the door. She locked it behind her and turned on the light.

Emet had cleaned thoroughly. The counters gleamed, and the chairs were back up on the tables. He had wiped down the blackboard, leaving the slate clean. Except…a single sentence remained, down in the corner. Eden Rose turned on another light and squatted to see.

In Emet's angular hand she read,

I try to tell the truth.

Eden Rose stood and turned off the extra light. She went behind the counter and began to tally up the day's receipts. A smile curved her mouth.

6

"So then what's the difference between a patient and a client?" said Emet. He and his date were tucking into a late dinner at the local microbrewery. It was far enough from the center of town that few tourists found it, and even fewer locals would have revealed its existence to them. The burgers were juicy, the fries crisp on the outside and creamy within; and the house dessert, proudly displayed on a counter near the kitchen, was a multilayered chocolate cake the size of a hatbox. Its secret ingredient, which was not even remotely secret, was the house stout. Waitresses in blue jeans and dangly earrings carried plates through clouds of conversation. The air was thick with the scent of French fries, and the walls were rough boards from a two hundred year-old barn that had blown down in a hurricane named Floyd some years earlier.

"It's a different kind of relationship," she said. "Seeing as they come to me for treatment."

"Which makes them patients."

"Clients, I could be installing storm windows for them."

"Or upgrading the photo copier."

"Right. Patient is something specific."

"Do they call you 'Doctor'?"

"I go by my first name."

"Dr. Mercedes."

"Mercey. And that would sound too stupid with 'Doctor.'"

"But you are one. Right?"

"Not in the way you're thinking." She tucked her sparrow-brown hair behind her ears and stabbed a tomato with her fork. "Me, I never wanted the MD. But I have the doctorate in physical therapy, so you better believe I'm a doctor."

"What's the difference?"

"I'm a doctor of movement dysfunction. You get in a car accident and shatter your legs, the MDs stitch you up. Then they send you to me so you can learn how to walk again."

"Or press a button with my nose because I'm paralyzed from the neck down."

"Or whatever," she agreed. "I teach people how their bodies work so they can heal themselves."

"That's really cool." Emet's voice was casual, but under the table his right foot twitched as though independent of him. "How long have you been doing that?"

"Graduated in May, started work in June."

"Is it something you always wanted to do?"

Mercey chatted easily. She was a small woman with round, dark eyes and full cheeks. Her nose was straight until the very tip, where it bent just enough to be charmingly beaky. Her lips were plump, and she smiled easily. The light from the Tiffany-style lamp over their booth was bright enough to show that she wore no makeup. Her skin was clear, her waist was small, and her hair fell past her shoulders in wings. She exuded health without vanity. Mercedes Finch was the kind of woman who, as a teenager, had probably been baffled when boys had crushes on her.

"Probably since high school," she said. "I was always really good in science, and I knew I wanted a job working with people. I mean, senior year I took, like, four science courses. Bio and chem and anatomy and physiology—my mom freaked out. She wanted me to learn typing so I could be a secretary. Then when I kept taking science," she laughed at her mother's defeat, "she told me to get a nursing degree so I could get a job."

"What does she think now?"

"Well, she knows I have a job," said Mercey. "I was kind of cruel in grad school, though. I kept telling her about cutting open cadavers and stuff."

"You were cutting open cadavers?"

"We shared them with Yale med school. That was when the dropouts left the program. I just giggled."

"Where do they get the bodies?" said Emet. "I always wondered about that."

"People donate them. You know, in their wills. It used to be criminals."

Emet stopped with a French fry halfway to his mouth. "Seriously?"

Mercey nodded, her mouth full. "Long time ago," she said as she swallowed. "And if there weren't enough criminals, anatomy profs would send their students out to dig up graves." She picked up a fry and bit it. "Extra credit!"

"So some guy's been executed and his family can't even get his body back for a burial?"

"I don't know," she said. "Maybe once the med school was done with it. I never thought about it before." She reached for another. "What do you do?"

Emet took a sip of water. "I work at a coffee shop near Worthington. Serve You Right. I mean, that's what it's called. Know it?"

"I think so," she said. "Do they have a striped awning in the summer and dog biscuits out front?"

"Right on."

"I must have walked past it a million times."

"You should stop in some time."

"I'll bring my dog," she said. "What do you do there?"

"Little of everything. My boss lets me experiment a lot in the kitchen. I make a wicked croissant."

"You're a chef." She smiled in a way that made her nose crinkle.

Emet flashed a return smile. "Chef is kind of overstating it, I think."

"Was it something you always wanted?" She pecked at her salad with her fork.

"I was a busboy for a while out of high school," said Emet. "I didn't get into the cooking aspect till recently."

"What did you do before then?"

"A bunch of different things," he said. "I liked the cooking best. So do you work with people in their homes, or what?"

"I could." Mercey wiped her mouth with her napkin. "The DPT is really flexible. But right now I do outpatient at a clinic."

"What's that like?"

"I love it," she said. "It's really fast-paced. I see a new patient every half hour. I get twenty-five minutes for lunch, and they give me half an hour for paperwork. Other than that I'm with my patients, teaching them about nutrition, exercise, hydration. And I know you were kidding about pressing a button with your nose, but sometimes that's for real."

"I bet," said Emet. "Do you always work this late?"

"Depends on the day," said Mercey. "It's a forty-hour week, but sometimes I go in early or stay late. We're open till 9:30 so we can get people after work. Tonight was my late night."

Emet shook his head. "So do you, like, live on caffeine? Because I'm listening to this and all I can think is, 'She must have every coffee shop in town on speed dial.'"

"What kind of a PT would I be if I ignored my own health?" protested Mercey. "I get enough sleep. And I have my jailbird buddy to help me out when I'm feeling frazzled."

Emet hiccupped on his water. "Um. Did you say jailbird?"

Mercedes laughed as she lifted her burger. "My dog. She's a therapy dog in training. I have her on weekends, but the rest of the time she's in the big house."

"The big house."

"Yup."

Emet's foot stopped twitching. "She's in a prison-based dog-training program."

"Oh, you've heard of those." Mercey was delighted. "Usually I have to explain."

"I've heard of them," said Emet. He kept his eyes on his drink. "So, how much is the dog with you?"

"I get her every Friday, and bring her back Sunday night. I keep telling her she's on furlough."

"Oh."

"Or parole."

Emet gave a smile that did not reach his eyes. "What's that like for you, going into a prison every week?"

"Oh, I don't. Just the foyer. They bring her out to me."

"Still. What's it like?"

"Honestly? It's creepy." She put her burger down on her plate and wiped her fingers on her napkin. "It's a medium-security men's facility. I went there for volunteer orientation last winter, and I guess I was thinking, you know, *medium*. It sounds so middle-of-the-road. And then I came around the corner and I saw it for the first time—you have to picture this."

"Okay," said Emet.

"Grey barracks," she said. "Towers with floodlights, and a fence inside a fence inside a fence, all topped with huge coils of razor wire. And it was night, and it was raining, and it was windy, so the rain was blowing in these huge waves." Her hands soared to describe the scene. "It looked like something from an old gangster movie. And I thought," here her eyes grew round and her hands gripped an invisible steering wheel, *"'I think I'm in the right place.'"*

A small glint appeared in Emet's eye. "Home, sweet home."

"What?"

"For the guys that live there," he said. "Do you ever meet them? The ones who train your dog?"

She shook her head. "I only know what I see in her."

"Meaning?"

"Serena is a great dog."

"Even with her rough neighborhood?"

"Probably because of it," said Mercey. "Look, I joke about it too. I keep saying I ought to dress her in black and white stripes. But the reality is, it's easy to ruin a dog. It's hard to raise one. Those men—I don't think they got where they are by accident—"

"Meaning what?"

Mercey gave him an appraising look. "Meaning they've been convicted of very serious crimes, a lot of them," she said finally.

"Doesn't that bother you?"

"That's not my end of things."

"No," he said. "I guess not."

"And look," she went on. "Whatever else they've done, they're training a really sweet pup, and someday she'll leave them and spend the rest of her life helping people. That's got to count for something in the scheme of things."

"Redemption."

"I guess."

Emet leaned into the cone of lamplight. "Do you feel like you see the good in them in her?"

"I never thought about it that way."

"But you could?"

"It's beautiful," said Mercey. "I'm going to use that."

When they had paid their tab, Mercedes stood up and shrugged her purse onto her shoulder. "Walk me home?" she said.

Emet blinked. "Do you want me to?"

"You don't seem like a rapist or a crazy stalker dude, and my car's in the shop."

Emet laughed as he held open the door for her. "Way to make a guy feel special, Dr. Finch."

Mercey's house was a split-level with a low, grey roof and concrete stairs leading in two directions, up and down. A fluorescent carriage lantern illuminated the front door in unnatural pallor, and a surly, yellow light smudged a basement window.

She and Emet had talked for most of their walk, sometimes flirting and sometimes not. Glittering threads of meaning ran through their conversation. When they lapsed into silence, the silences were smooth and perfect. Neither groped for the wrong word or clenched at awkward pauses. And neither cared to disengage from this marvelous new entity they were creating with their voices and their steps and their hands swinging at their sides, not quite touching one another.

"My brother's home," she said as they walked up the broken bricks of the walkway.

Emet had been silent for the last block. Now he started, because everything in Mercey had abruptly shifted, as though she were banking on wind shears no one could see.

"You live with your brother?" he said.

"It's our mom's house, so up till last month I guess you could say we lived with her."

"What happened last month?"

"She has MS." Mercey stopped at the base of the stairs that led up. "Long story short, she needs more help than I can give her, so as of four weeks ago she's in assisted living and she hates it, and I'm moving out in a couple of days but I'm not sure my brother knows because" she drew a breath, "he has trouble remembering stuff when he's stoned." Something in her expression was both tentative and defiant.

"Ah," said Emet after a pause. "How often is that?"

"Not sure," she said. "He'd have to be straight occasionally so I could compare." She gave a hard, chirping laugh.

"Wow," said Emet.

"The fun never stops," said Mercey. Her voice was unnaturally bright.

Emet looked at her. She glared as if daring him to agree with her, or to disagree. But he said nothing and he did not look away, and presently her shoulders slumped.

"I'm sorry," she said, and her eyes dipped to the pavement.

"We all have stuff," he said. "Everybody's got stuff."

"I shouldn't have said anything."

Emet thrust his hands into the pockets of his jacket and rocked on the balls of his feet. "Well. I think I get why you're moving."

She half laughed. "Yeah. Sunday."

"New place, new start?" Emet gestured, his hands still in his pockets, so his jacket flapped around him. "New lease on life?"

"God, I hope so."

He cleared his throat. "Are you going to be far away?"

"I'll be sharing an apartment with a girlfriend from work." She looked at him oddly. "Couple miles from here. Why?"

Emet glanced at the walkway. Weeds grew between the bricks. "Need any help moving?"

A smile flew to her face, and a rush of surprise and relief flitted across her cheeks and eyes. "That would be great."

Emet nodded. "I have a car—let me know when."

Deep in the shaggy lawn, invisible crickets plied their bows, layering the night with sparkling chants.

"I had a good time tonight." Mercey broke the silence. "And listen, about just now—it's just that I thought he was going to be out. Took me by surprise."

"No worries."

"Usually I wait till the second date till I go all weird like that."

"Second date?"

"Yes."

Emet smiled. "Does helping you move count as a second date? I mean, if I bring pizza?"

"Sure." Her own smile seemed to have taken up permanent residence; now it filled her voice.

"Good."

"Sure you want to?" Mercey spoke carefully, giving him the option to leave if he chose.

"Just said I would."

"I have stuff," she said. "And not just the kind that fits in boxes."

"Who doesn't?"

"You seem pretty comfortable in your own skin."

"Everyone has a past," he said. "No one has the future. We all have now, and right now, I like what I see."

"Cute. Thanks." She put her hands in her pockets so their profiles mirrored each other. "So, Confucius, what's your secret?"

"What?"

"What's your dark and dirty past that makes you so accepting?"

Emet breathed though his nose. "I think maybe that's second date material too."

He said nothing more, but he stopped moving.

Mercey set her expression to default: friendly. "Okay. Can't wait to hear." She turned to walk up the stairs to the front door. "Call me about Sunday," she said over her shoulder.

"Good night."

"G'night."

Emet walked away from the light, then swiveled back. He gripped the iron railing at the side of the steps. His face was sickly in the artificial white of the fluorescent lamp. "Mercey," he said, and his voice was dusky with panic.

She drew back. "What?"

"Everybody has stuff they're not proud of," he said. The words tumbled.

She stiffened almost imperceptibly. "Okay. So?"

"I'm not—a rapist or a crazy stalker dude," he said. His eyes blazed with dark fear. "But there is something."

Mercedes lowered herself to the concrete step and cocked her head at the empty space next to her. Emet sat by her side, not facing her. When he turned away from the lantern, his features were edged with shadows as sharp as blades. He rubbed his fingers across his knuckles.

She waited.

"Okay," he said. "This was about ten years ago. I was at work, that busboy job I told you about. Diner, big place. A lot of guys worked there, mostly guys I knew. It was the kind of neighborhood where the kids all grew up together and everybody's in everybody's business. I mean, our moms all knew each other and stuff. Anyway." He cleared this throat. "Anyway."

Emet glanced at Mercey. Her dark eyes rested on him, their clarity heightened by the light of the lantern. He looked away again. "So—this one day, I come into the kitchen with my load, and I hear two of the guys talking smack about some girl they know. Only as soon as I come in, my friend Vic yells at them to shut up. Then he tells me they're a couple of jerks. He says besides, I've known Jade since the eighth grade, and she'd never do something like that. Which is the first clue I have that they're talking about *my girlfriend.*"

"Your girlfriend," said Mercey.

"Yeah. So I'm like, 'What the hell?' and Vic says, 'E, I wasn't gonna say anything, but Jake,' that's one of the guys that was talking, 'Jake hit on her and she turned him down, and he's been badmouthing her ever since. Just making shit up.' But I looked at him, and I knew he was lying." He paused, looking at his hands. Mercedes was silent.

"Up till then," said Emet, "I never would have thought of her that way. I mean, I never saw her look at another guy. And besides, we were like the same person half the time, you know? We'd finish each other's sentences. Or I'd have a song going through my head and she'd start singing it right where it was for me. But I—when I heard those guys talking about her that way, it…."

He trailed off. Several blocks over, traffic growled. Emet sighed. "They were talking about her the way guys talk when they've—gotten away with something. That's why I couldn't get it out of my head. So end of the day I go home, and I ask her, is she cheating on me? And she *cries* and says no, no, how could I say that and all. And I tell her I don't believe her, which wasn't exactly true. It was just I didn't know what to believe.

And she's just crying like a maniac and she won't let me touch her. And the more she cries the more I yell. So I leave the apartment, and I walk around the neighborhood for, I don't know, hours. And I was so mad I felt like anything I touched would just explode. But after a while, you know? I thought, this is crazy. Every relationship has its ups and downs. I love her and she loves me, I've known her since the eighth grade, and whatever problems we're having we'll fix them. So I go home to tell her all that. And she's in bed with Vic."

Mercedes shut her eyes in acknowledgement. "Oh, God."

Emet stared at a place a long time away. "Even then I don't think I would have—done anything—if he hadn't tried to run past me. But I was in the doorway and that was the only way out. So he runs for it and he's got this big, shit-eating grin and he's grabbing the sheets around him. And I lost it."

Mercey's hands lay still, clasped in her lap.

"Just—knowing he was lying and she was lying and they were laughing at me the whole time—and he would run away and leave her there with me like she's just this thing he's done using—I grabbed a lamp and hit him hard as I could." His arm twitched. "Just, *pow!* You know? And my whole arm goes numb, and the room goes dark, 'cause it was the only light on. Then my girlfriend, she turns on another light, and she makes this little noise. Not a big scream, like they do on TV, you know? Just this little sound, like she was swallowing something. And he's lying there. And I'm holding the lamp."

Mercey breathed into the silence. Finally she said, "Was he…?"

"A few seconds later. He looked at me and I saw his eyes glass over. And I thought—you know how they tell you in school we're all, what, sixty cents' worth of chemicals or whatever it is? And I looked at him and all I can think is, 'Oh, God. Vic's gone. All that's left is sixty cents of chemicals.'" He looked down. Mercey waited.

"Did you run?" she said presently.

He shook his head. "Told Jade to call 911. Running—I can't imagine living that way, looking over your shoulder every second. Nah." He sighed. "So the cops came and the ambulance came and they took me away in handcuffs. And that was the last time I ever saw my girlfriend."

"She wasn't at the trial?"

"I didn't have a trial," said Emet. "Didn't see the point, seeing as I was guilty. So I pleaded to manslaughter and did my time, and—now I'm out."

There was a long pause. Presently, Mercey nodded. "Okay."

Emet turned to look at her. "What?"

"I figured it was something like that."

"How?"

"You had ten missing years," she said. "You said you had the busboy job out of high school, and you're what, thirty?"

"Thirty-one."

"And the job you're in now sounds like an entry-level position too, but in the same field. It didn't make sense that you would take ten years to get from busboy to cook. And then you got so serious when I told you about my dog. Usually people joke about it. So I figured you'd probably done time."

"You're smart," he said. "No one else has figured that out."

"I have a pretty good bullshit detector," she said. "My patients hate that about me."

The shadows on Emet's face darkened. "I didn't—"

"I'm sorry," she interrupted. "That sounded terrible, and I didn't mean it that way. It's just—I'm in the business of figuring people out. So I notice gaps."

"I'm on parole," he said. "I'm still serving my sentence, just on the outside. And if I violate the terms of my release, they can pull me back for the rest of my time."

Mercedes leaned back against the railing. "What does that entail?"

"Obey the law, get a job, see my parole officer. No drugs or alcohol."

"You had water with dinner."

"Yup."

"Doesn't sound too bad."

"And I pee into a lot of cups," said Emet. "They're crazy for my pee."

"Drugs."

"I never did drugs."

"Good."

"Could be worse," said Emet. "Some guys get a curfew."

"Hey," said Mercey. "Were you ever in a dog-training program?"

"No. But I knew guys who were. A lot of the lifers do it."

"I was just wondering if you knew my dog."

Emet shook his head. "I was near Boston."

"You're a long way from home." She tilted her head as if she could see the mountains that embraced the town, as if she could smell the sharp, woody smell of the pines that had once fed a line of brick mills along the river.

"As far as I could get and still be in the state," he said. "I couldn't go home again. Vic's mom still lives in the neighborhood. And I didn't want to see Jade."

"Are you still in love with her?"

"No. I just don't want to see her."

A truck went by, driving too fast. In the distance a siren howled. When Emet spoke, his voice was laden with darkness. "So now you know."

"Yes."

He stood. "If you want to know more, you can Google me. Most of what they said was pretty accurate." He turned to go.

Mercey stood. "Emet. Can I see you again?"

He gave her a look of swift, bright happiness. "Sure. Call me."

"It would help if I had your phone number."

"God." Emet pulled out his wallet and handed her a card. "No, wait." He took it back and scribbled a number on the back. "This one's my home phone. The other is work."

Mercedes looked at the card. *Serve You Right A Neighborhood Coffee Shop 100 Railroad Street Oxbridge MA.* The number, hours, and website were listed next to a cartoon of a steaming coffee mug. "No cell phone?"

"No credit card," he said. "But I'm working on it." He smiled again and left, a light in his step.

9

Mercey opened the door and strode into her house. A shadow that wasn't a shadow slopped on the sofa.

"So now you're fucking an ex-con," said the shadow. "Classy."

"Clay?" Mercey hit the wall switch. White light filled the room, revealing a plaid sofa and a coffee table covered with fast-food wrappers. A man with light-brown hair to match her own lay on the sofa. He flung an arm over his eyes when the light hit him. "What the hell?" she said. "Were you listening?"

"Window was open, and you weren't whispering," said Clay. He lowered his arm to squint at her. "Hey, do you mind turning that down, for fuck's sake?"

Clay was older than Mercedes by four minutes. He was a giant kludge of a man, tall and fleshy, with a round face. Nothing about him seemed to fit anything else. He wore a red shirt from a video arcade; inside it his shoulders sloped as though they had eroded. He and she had the same round eyes, but whereas hers were quick and bright, his had the dullness of plastic marbles. His nose was hooked like an eagle's, or had been before he broke it. A miasma of beer, pot smoke, and week-old tee shirt clung to him.

"Did you pick up my car?" she said.

"You want some stoner driving your car?" he said. "That is so fucking irresponsible."

"You said you'd get it for me."

"Don't try to change the subject. Who's the new guy?"

"Jesus Christ, asshole, where is my car?"

He furrowed his brow. "That's a very good question. Where do you last remember seeing it? This could be an important clue."

"At the garage, after you ran it up on the curb and blew out the tires."

"Oh, that's right. That was very dangerous, wasn't it? I wonder if drugs were involved."

"Fucking hell, Clay, this isn't funny. Did you get it or not?"

"Don't try to change the subject, Doctor Doctor. Who's the new guy? Is he a double dollop of drop-dead gorgeous? All's I could see was the back of his head."

"Clay—"

"Is he a good fuck?"

"Shut the hell up."

"Does he know about you?"

Mercedes looked like a bird that cannot fly away. "Know what about me?"

"You're the fucking Godzilla of relationships. You smash guys' balls like Tokyo. You're a mutant dinosaur stomping on stupid guys while the smart ones run away screaming in Japanese."

Mercey closed her eyes. "Clay. I need my car. Did you get it from the garage or not?"

Clay considered a spot on the ceiling. "No," he said finally. "I did not."

"Why the hell not?"

"It seemed imprudent."

"Goddamn it, you said you'd get it for me today."

"So get it Monday."

"I need it this weekend!"

"What's the rush, Doctor Doctor? Got a road trip planned?"

"I'm moving out Sunday, moron."

Clay regarded her impassively. "I think that will be very difficult without a car."

Mercey looked at her brother with shuddering revulsion. "Clay. I'm leaving on Sunday. You can't stop me."

"Shut up," said Clay lazily.

"You'll have to handle the bills and the insurance and the termite bond."

"Fuck you."

"The city is coming Monday to dig up the water main, so you'll be without water for a few days."

"Shut up *and* fuck you. Leave me alone." Clay peered at her. His eyes looked like cigarette burns in a blanket. "Are you moving in with that guy?"

"Jesus, Clay, I just met him. I told you about the move weeks ago."

"Weeks ago." Clay repeated the phrase carefully, as though examining it for snap traps.

"I'm getting an apartment with my friend from work."

"The ex-con with the big dick."

"My *girlfriend*. Why do you think he's part of this?"

"Because I just can't see you taking a great big step like that all by your little self, Doctor Doctor. You're always so good and so well-behaved. And you promised Mom you'd stay here."

"I never said that."

"Pants on *fire.*"

"Goddamn it, Clay, I told Mom I wouldn't kick you out. I promised her you could stay here as long as I was here. And now I'm leaving because I can't afford to pay for Mom and her care, and the taxes and upkeep on this house, and you and your goddamn drug habit."

A bruise-colored silence stretched between them.

"When did you turn into such a liar?" said Clay at last. "Was it when you met this guy and started playing doctor, Doctor Doctor?" He sat up, scowling. "Is he a good patient? Does he do everything you say?"

A scrabbling sound came from overhead. Mercey's eyes flicked at the ceiling. "Did you let Serena out?"

"You care more about that bitch than you do about me, bitch."

Mercey opened her hands in defeat. "Fine, Clay. You win. Last month I secretly planned to leave you in the lurch because I love my dog more than I love you, and also so I could move in with a guy I hadn't met yet. I covered my tracks by telling you all about it and breaking a promise I never made. You foiled my scheme by wrecking my car and not picking it up at the garage. Now I'll stay here forever, paying bills and keeping house for my loser junkie brother because I've never heard of renting a moving van." She turned toward the stairs.

"You have a mean streak, Doctor Doctor," called Clay. "Do your patients love that about you?"

She did not answer. Her shoes tapped along the short hallway; her door opened and shut. A whine of joy lit up the night, and Mercey's voice murmured cozy songs.

"Shut up," Clay whispered at the ceiling. "Fuck you. Leave me alone."

Shaking, he covered his face with his hands. His foot stomped on the worn rug, and his knee knocked against the coffee table. He mumbled into his palms without syllables.

If he could have spoken his rage and passion, he would have said, “This house was my primeval world. It is where I first saw and heard and felt and dreamed. It is where I was when our father left, and before that, when I thought I was loved. This house is draped in memories of protection for me. They may be false, but they are mine. If you leave me here, our home will die. I cannot care for it, and if it dies I will too.”

Clay took his hands away from his face and stared at the ceiling where his sister lived. “Mom would have never done this to me,” he said softly.

When Mercey walked down the stairs a few minutes later with her German shepherd on a leash and a plastic bag stuffed halfway into her pocket, the living room was empty. The door to the basement stairs was open, and the livid clacking of Clay's keyboard rattled the air. Mercey opened the door and walked into the relief of the night.

Downstairs, in his cave of shadows and secrets, Clay typed furiously into his favorite chat room.

> *Status: betrayed. U will not believe this. After my mom made my sister promise I cd stay here she is leaving. Now what am I supposd to do?*

Two faces came up in the bar above the chat screen, grinning, pixilated images whose movements did not quite match reality.

> *WHITE DRAGON: Yr mom is leaving? Thought she already left.*
>
> *ADAM BOMBED: No moron. He means his sister is leaving right Claymation?*

Clay took a swig from a can next to his keyboard and typed.

CLAYMATION: Yeah I mean my sister. Shit she has a job and it is a good one. She cd afford to stay. I got my own problems. Why should she get more out of life than I do? I desrv better than this. I have been the man of the family since my dad left. Nobody gets a free ride but thats just what shes taking here.

ADAM BOMBED: Whoah. Treasonable offense, man.

WHITE DRAGON: Harsh.

ADAM BOMBED: Whats your plan Claymation?

CLAYMATION: Make her keep her promise.

WHITE DRAGON: What promise?

CLAYMATION: Dragon no offense but you are a fucking moron. When my mom went into the home she made Mercey-less promise I could stay here. So I guess she knew or suspected this betrayal would come.

ADAM BOMBED: And now shes leaving. Typical.

WHITE DRAGON: Did your mom make her promise to stay? Or just promise to let you stay?

CLAYMATION: Jesus H Christ you idiot. Its the same thing. Honest to God if I didn't know you better I would think you were stoned or something.

ADAM BOMBED: Dragon Claymation is right. It amounts to the same thing. Sister-friend did an end run around her promise to her sick mother. That is sick. Hey, are you stoned?

WHITE DRAGON: I got so wasted last night I threw up on myself. Here's the picture.

ADAM BOMBED: Dude!

CLAYMATION: Thx for the support guys. Its good to know I can count on my friends when my sister turns out to be a backstabbing doublecrossing ironclad bitch from hell.

ADAM BOMBED: A woman will stick you in the back.

WHITE DRAGON: But an elephant's faithful, one hundred percent!

ADAM BOMBED: So maybe you should get an elephant.

CLAYMATION: Thx for the Dr. Seuss, White Dragon. I was hoping for Shakespeare or Cicero but in this economy Ill take what I can get.

Clay got up from his keyboard and walked rapidly in small, tight circles. He thumped his fist into his palm and landed heavy on his heels. He sat down again and took another swallow from the can, then leaned back and ran his fingers through his sweaty hair. A new message had appeared.

WHITE DRAGON: Hey Claymation. Radical notion but did you ever consider you could stop smoking weed and get a job?

CLAYMATION: Im disabled.

WHITE DRAGON: Dude no disrespect but you buy your disability in nickel bags every weekend.

ADAM BOMBED: Dragon you need to shut the fuck up. This is serious. Hey is all that puke for real or did you Photoshop it?

CLAYMATION: I can tell ur both bleeding for me. Did I tell you she is moving in with a convicted felon?

WHITE DRAGON: Convicted of what?

CLAYMATION: Murder. He killed a man with his bare hands.

WHITE DRAGON: Thank God. For a second I was afraid it might be drugs.

CLAYMATION: U r an asshole Dragon you know that?

ADAM BOMBED: Is this true? Mercy-less is cutting out on you so she can waste her youth on some ex-con?

CLAYMATION: Yes.

ADAM BOMBED: And you are letting her do this to you?

CLAYMATION: Fuck no.

ADAM BOMBED: She is majorly disrespecting you. Your mom said you could stay there. That makes it your house. Your house your rules and one of the rules is you dont let your sister bang some jaildirt. It makes you look bad.

CLAYMATION: Exactly.

WHITE DRAGON: And u r stopping her how? I bet all this messaging has her sweating blue bullets.

CLAYMATION: Shut up.

ADAM BOMBED: Clay-man, I will cut the shit for just long enough to tell you this: be a man.

WHITE DRAGON: I hate to say it but Adam is right. If you let her walk she will walk.

CLAYMATION: I KNOW THAT.

ADAM BOMBED: You have got to stand up for yourself.

CLAYMATION: How?

WHITE DRAGON: Adam B is having a good day. Hes right again. If you let her do this to you she will take advantage of you in ways you cant imagine.

CLAYMATION: So whats the strategy?

ADAM BOMBED: Use what's left of your brain moron. Stop this guy and she'll have no reason to go.

Clay nodded at the screen. He typed.

CLAYMATION: Done.

He got up and walked upstairs.

Clay opened the door to his sister's room. Her purse sat on the bureau. He pulled out her credit cards, cell phone, driver's license, and work ID, and the blue plastic folder containing her checkbook. He felt in the pocket behind the register and smiled as he pulled out a business card. He put it and the cell phone in his pocket, re-packed the purse, and left.

In the kitchen, he paused to glower at Serena's dog bowls. He emptied her water bowl, then refilled it from the tap. He grabbed a box of salt and upended it over the water. A white stream like a special-effects waterfall hissed into the dog dish. He whipped the water with a fork until the granules disappeared. Then he put the dish back and retreated to his computer and his video games and the only people who really understood how hard his life was.

Saturday, September 20

Hours of Operation:

8:00 am to 5:00 pm

Eden Rose awoke to plum-colored clouds crowding a sky shot with silver. She cranked open her windows. The air smelled of rain, thick and sweet as maple syrup. A tepid breeze unspooled a thread of cold, a harbinger of frost and black ice. But it also carried autumn: wet pavement and earth, and a hint of the orchards outside town, hanging heavy with the warm spice of fall. Leaves stirred, the colors of wine and gold; berries were luster-glossed. The shower had already drenched them. They quaked at the tapping of raindrops, and their taps added to the susurration of the rain. As Eden Rose drew a breath of the thick air, the first drops reached her and spatted against the glass.

A sun catcher hanging in the multicolored shadows bumped her shoulder. In flowing script it read, "And the Wisdom to Know the Difference."

A warm growl and a touch of silk against her ankles made her look down. Her cats, Midnight and Nyx, twined around her in a restless figure eight, looking up at her with their flat, expressionless faces. “Are you trying to tell me something?” she said.

They went into the kitchen, where bags of apples bulged against the walls. Eden Rose set out food and fresh water for the cats. Leaning against the wall, she watched them over a steaming mug of coffee whose sharp perfume mingled with the apple-scented air.

“So what do you think?” she said to the cats. “Emet do okay on his date?”

Nyx flicked his tail.

“You’re right,” said Eden. “He’ll tell me if he wants to.” She sat at her farm-style table and pulled a pen and writing pad toward her. Across the top a flowing script proclaimed, “A Good Meal Is a Promise Kept.” Eden Rose uncapped the pen and began to write the day.

Something angry hit Mercey’s window. She opened her eyes.

This, her mother’s house, was the only home Mercey had ever known. This room had been her egg and her nest. The walls were hung with framed awards for academics and archery and swimming, and the bookcase held trophies for Math League and Science Decathlon. A laptop computer sat open on her desk, over which was a bulletin board edged with blue ribbons for high school gymnastics. Clay and her mother had come to precisely none of her events.

The carpet had been pink when she was a little girl; now it was the color of crushed roses, blotchy and uneven. Boxes covered much of it. Some were taped shut; others flapped open like fledglings demanding to be fed. They were labeled: "PT books" and "Shoes" and "Novels" and "More Shoes" and "PT Books #2" and "Holy Crap, How Did I Get So Many Shoes?" Leaning against her desk was her briefcase, thick with paperwork that didn't fit into the daily half-hour the clinic budgeted for it. Half the hangers in her closet hung empty and askew, but some still held lab coats. One pair of sparkly pumps, never worn, gleamed darkly in the depths.

Next to the bed was the room's most luxurious feature, a Tempur-Pedic dog bed in glorious denim and fleece. Curled up in it, Serena lifted her head and peered at Mercedes. Her face remained grave as only a German shepherd's can, but her tail thumped in morning glee.

The enraged tapping came again. Mercey glided to the window, keeping her movements smooth. He was back.

For the past several weeks, a catbird had been attacking this window with a furious optimism undimmed by its abject failure rate. Its head was capped with black, its body the color of November rain. As Mercey approached, the bird stopped its onslaught and turned its head to glare at her with a single, glittering eye. She stopped, letting her stillness calm him. The bird unruffled its feathers and stopped twitching. Its unreadable eye was dark and bright, like onyx.

"I don't mean to feed into stereotypes," she told it, "but there's a reason smart people aren't called 'birdbrain.'"

The catbird flapped to a twig three feet away and launched itself at the house with renewed vigor. The window's strategy (stand still and let the bird smack into it) proved superior, and the bird dropped to the sill, fluttering its wings back into place and jerking its head, the image of wounded dignity.

Mercedes quoted a line she used with her patients. "If you do what you always did, you'll get what you always got."

The catbird cocked its head. Behind it, rain began to storm into the leaves of the big maple that shaded the house. The drops were grey as iron, and in seconds they came down hard, like a gate slamming shut.

The catbird considered the window, Mercedes, and the rain, then flickered away in a manner that left no doubt it would be back for revenge later.

Mercey touched the crosshatched bars on the window, something she could not have done without frightening the catbird away. “I don’t get you,” she told its absence. “Why are you trying so hard to get in when I’m doing my damndest to break out?”

Emet’s room was plain. The walls were Frigidaire white and undecorated; he had a bed and a table with a phone and an answering machine. His mother called him once a week, as he had phoned her each of the five hundred weeks of his incarceration. Now they could talk for more than twenty minutes, and he didn’t need to call collect.

Next to the answering machine, a shoebox held a dozen or so letters in plain, white envelopes. The return addresses were in different handwritings, but each one was stamped the same: “This correspondence is forwarded from a Massachusetts Correctional Institution. The contents may not have been evaluated and the Department of Correction is not responsible for the substance or content of the enclosed material.” Emet had answered all of them. *Did you see the game last week? Say hi to the guys for me.* He was almost out of stamps and envelopes.

After almost ten years of enforced early rising, Emet could not sleep late. He was awake and smiling before the first drops hit his windows. The rain fell hard, and soon water was chuckling in the drainpipe. "Awesome," he said to no one, and lifted the casement to watch the world being washed clean.

Emet's apartment was on the second floor of an oatmeal-colored building with a green, metal roof. It was part of a low-income development, inside Oxbridge's city limits but far from the center of town where tourists congregated and natives took yoga classes and agreed with each other in the Unitarian Church. A strip mall in the next block took care of most of his shopping needs. Emet's car, a second-hand Subaru Outback, rested in its space in the parking lot. It and a driving test at the DMV had been his mother's gifts to him upon his release from prison. ("He hasn't had an accident in ten years," she proudly told the tester.) Sometimes he drove to work, because he could. Today he would walk in the rain. Because he could.

Emet's windbreaker had a hood, but he let it hang down his back as he stepped outside ten minutes later. Mist gathered on his cheeks and coalesced into warm droplets. Rain was the caress of an untouchable sky.

When he reached the center of town, Emet took a shortcut through the half-lot behind the Serve You Right Café. Eden Rose had planted herbs there: basil and rosemary and flat-leaf parsley, and mint confined to a barrel lest it run amok and take over the small garden. One of the coffee shop's signature cold-weather dishes was a mug of beef broth infused with mint leaves. Some of the regulars were already asking for it, but Eden Rose would not make winter food until after the first hard frost. "For every thing there is a season," she had told one customer.

"Turn, turn, turn," he had replied as she handed him his coffee.

The leaves were silvered over with rain. Emet ran his hand through them and lifted it to his face, inhaling to the fullest capacity of his lungs. The rain smelled like herbs and the herbs smelled like rain, and he exhaled as slowly as he could.

When he walked in the front door of the Serve You Right Café, Eden Rose was standing on a chair writing on the blackboard. *Worst Pun Ever. Free Refills with Every Groaner.* She stepped off and glanced at her watch.

"You're only fifteen minutes early," she said. "That's as close to late as you've ever been."

"Sorry, boss," he smiled. "Won't happen again." He shook his windbreaker outside the door before hanging it up on a peg. He walked behind the counter and put on his apron, stuffing his hair into the net.

"So?" said Eden Rose. "How did it go?"

Emet lit up. He had the dazzled look of a man who had, in the course of a single, enchanted interlude, cracked a secret code, won the lottery, and flawlessly assembled a dresser from

IKEA. “Great,” he said. “She’s smart, she’s funny, she’s gorgeous, and holy God, I think she likes me.”

Clay's mail beeped, and he woke up and rubbed his eyes. The screen was still on Duke Nukem 3D. It was Clay's favorite game, though Halo and Grand Theft Auto jostled it for space in the pantheon. Clay and Duke had spent much of the night killing monsters and aliens and prostitutes, or various combinations thereof. The mutant women begged, "Kill me," which made Clay show his teeth in a sliver. And every time he shot a stripper, a shower of dollar bills appeared. Clay barely moved when playing Duke Nukem, but he grunted every time he destroyed someone. Sometimes he got killed, but dead was just a temporary setback. Clay always came back with a new plan.

He opened his mail. The new message was from Adam Bombed.

R u gonna do this thing?

Clay belched, and a cloud of beer and stomach acid filled the basement room. He typed.

U bet.

Adam's answer came back.

Stick to the script, man. Tell him he can't fuck with you, then hit hard and run.

Clay replied.

Tell u all about it when im done.

He opened WhitePages.com, and pulled Emet's card out of his pocket. He typed the phone number with one finger and hit return. An address came up. He entered it into the map on Mercey's phone, and a blue walking route blinked onto the streets.

"You gonna make me walk, sonofabitch?" he said. "Don't you know it's fucking raining?" He went back to the chat room and typed, "Asshole duznt evn care if its raining." When no answer came, he pulled on his sneakers and stumped up the stairs.

Nothing in Oxbridge was very far from anything else, and twenty minutes later Clay was banging on Emet's door.

"Yo, First," he shouted. His brown hair stuck to his forehead, and rain thrummed on the portico roof. "Come on out, ya fuckin' loser."

The door opened and a Yeatsean figure appeared. A shock of white hair fell almost to his eyes, and he wore a tweed jacket with scuffed, leather elbow patches. One hand held an empty pipe. His fingers were slender and artistic.

"Yes?" he said.

Clay blinked. He looked at his sister's phone, and the house number next to the door. "Where's Emet First?"

"Not in, I'm afraid. You've missed him by a considerable margin." The voice was plummy, and spoke of Dickensian streets wreathed in fog and poetry.

"Huh?"

"He's gone to work," said the older man. He leaned against the doorjamb and tapped his fingers against the empty bowl of his pipe. "What business brings you to him on this dreary day?"

Clay scowled and jammed the phone into his pocket. His jacket dripped streams of water onto the portico floor, and his sneakers squelched when he shifted his weight. "That bas—guy…."

He stopped. The rain mumbled. Clay lifted his head and stared past the man.

"Sir?"

Clay's expression clicked as though he had been reset. His brows lifted so his eyes were open and engaging. His jaw relaxed; he smiled. "Hey. Can I trust you with a secret?"

A gleam of deep amusement appeared in the old man's eyes. "I would stake our entire friendship on it." He placed his pipe in his mouth and assumed the air of one who has settled in for a long listen.

Clay leaned in close. The man's nostrils flared at the barrage of smells, but he did not back away. "Emet's my customer," said Clay.

"I see."

"We have a joke," said Clay. "He's my *First* customer." He grinned.

The man removed his pipe from his mouth. "And what, may I ask, do you sell, sir?"

Clay glanced over his shoulder at the rain spattering onto a sodden stripe of lawn that ringed the building. No one else was outside. "Promise me you're no narc, man."

"My word is my bond, sir. I am not now, nor have I ever been, a narc."

"Skag," said Clay.

The man's eyes narrowed. "Are we speaking of heroin, sir?"

"Best junk ever, man!" Clay bounced. His shoes squeaked wetly. "So—my man Emet's out? You got a key to his place?"

"And why would you want to get into his flat, given that you know he's not there?"

"He'll pay me later." Clay reached into one of the pockets of his jacket and pulled a plastic bag partway out.

"How very accommodating of you," said the man. "Are all your colleagues so flexible regarding payment?"

Clay jammed the bag back into his pocket. "'Course not. But Emet's my man, so I'll just leave the stuff soon as you let me in." He shifted toward the doorway.

The taller man straightened so that he filled the entrance. He put his pipe in his pocket. "Emet doesn't use drugs," he said.

"I was as shocked as you when I found out." Clay's voice radiated appalled sincerity. "Him and his cleaned-up act."

"I don't believe it to be an act."

"Oh, yeah. Emet's—" Clay groped for a phrase. "—high-functioning."

"In what sense?"

Clay rolled his eyes. "It means only *functions* when he's *high*. Trust me—you never seen him when he's not skeeted up."

The old man said nothing. His gaze was as lucid as rainwater.

"It's the truth." Clay's voice rose. "Ever seen him dope sick?"

The man folded his long arms across his chest.

"Sick," said Clay. He was almost shouting. "Shaking, sweating, scared of the world. *Puking.*"

"No," said the man. "I have certainly never seen Emet in that condition."

"Know why?" Clay was breathing heavily, but his voice came down. "'Cos he's high all the time, man."

"I see."

"Fools everyone."

"Quite a performance."

"Emet's like that, you know, just naturally dishonest." Clay took a deep breath and spread his hands open wide. "Here's the reality, man. A junkie's a junkie. If Emet doesn't buy from me he'll get it from someone else. And I'm his friend, I'm looking out for him, you know? Making sure he gets the good stuff and not some damaging shit that could really hurt him."

The man's eyes traveled calmly over Clay's sodden form. "How do you know Emet?" he said finally.

Clay frowned thoughtfully. He brightened. "Cellmates."

"Really?"

"Oh, man. I guess I let the cat out of the bag," Clay sighed. He looked around at an invisible presence. "I'm real sorry, Emet—I thought you would of told people about that."

"He did," said the tall man.

Clay was outraged. "He *told* you? Jesus, what a moron."

"Be that as it may," said the tweed-jacketed man with the scuffed elbow patches, "I take it that you, too, sir, are a convicted felon?"

Clay drew himself up straight. "That's right. I mean, damn straight."

"Then perhaps it is unwise of you to be peddling controlled substances."

"I got bills to pay like anyone else."

"Has it occurred to you," said the old man, "that someone might report your activities to the narcs of whom you spoke earlier?"

They stared at each other. Neither one moved. There was a laziness to the tall man's bearing, and a shocked stolidity to Clay's.

"Fuck you," said Clay finally. "I could just punch your face in. I could."

The man's mouth tightened in a stern line. "You are a November man, sir. You are out of time, and your soul was crafted with fingers of fog."

"Shut up."

"You are ill-defined. You drift."

"Fuck you. Leave me alone."

"You drift," he repeated. "You lack the generosity of summer and the cold precision of winter."

"Shut *up.*" Clay's hand went to his chest. He gulped the air.

The old man removed his pipe from his pocket and placed it between his teeth, which were crooked and yellow. "I plan to," he said. Water drummed on the portico roof. "Hadn't you best be going, sir? I believe it is about to rain."

Clay stumped home, shoulders bunched and awkward. The sky was the color of torn dreams, and the clouds spat on him as he walked. The rain brought decay, washing down dead things in the air and the earth and the trees. The sidewalks smelled of mud and rust.

When he reached his basement he fell into his chair. Adam Bombed had left him a message.

Did u get him?

Clay's thick fingers jerked on the keyboard. He moved as though he were shot through with pain, like a scarecrow stuffed with broken glass.

CLAYMATION: No he got away from me the slick bastrd but it wont hapn again.

ADAM BOMBED: Got a plan?

"Duh," said Clay. His fingers twitched over the keys.

U bet I have a plan he wont be a problm when I am done with him

This will take care of that bastrd for good

He leaned back and watched the rain course down the windowpanes in sullen rivulets.

13

It was Saturday, and the flood of customers was less frantic than on weekdays. Ruthie, a petite and energetic student at Worthington, came in for her part-time job, and once she was ensconced behind the counter Emet retreated to the back to tinker with the beta version of the açai berry scones. Behind the counter and around a bend so as to be invisible to the paying public, this area comprised a kitchen, a larder, and Eden Rose's office. The door separating the two portions of the coffee shop was solid oak, but Eden Rose kept it well-oiled and it swung freely without a squeak.

The line was short when there was one, and a few chairs stood vacant. Mid-morning, a mother with her school-aged son and daughter came in for coffee and a yogurt parfait; her kids, after some soul-searching, decided on a blueberry muffin and a morning bun. They sat themselves at one of the round tables, their mother reminding them that once they were done with breakfast they all had homework to do. Their gusty sighs indicated that this fact had been previously established; but once they had eaten and cleared their places, the son settled down with a math packet, and the daughter pulled a bookmark out of *Magic Tree House #2: The Knight at Dawn.* The mother thumped a psychology textbook onto the table along with a notebook and highlighter.

More customers ambled in, took their orders, and sat at the tables. A few wrote their groaners on the board.

Know what Santa's elves are? A bunch of subordinate Clauses.

Three scientists walk into a bar. They forgot to duck.

How do you make holy water? Boil the hell out of it!

Emet came out from the back room, his forehead spangled with perspiration, and propped open the door. The rain had slowed, but moisture still hung in the air, and it was warm for September.

"So," said Eden Rose as she swabbed off a tabletop, "does Wonder Woman have a name?"

"Mercedes," said Emet. "She goes by Mercey."

"Are you seeing her again?"

"I'm helping her move tomorrow."

"You slick dude."

"What?"

"It's just one of those things people do for each other. You know, like driving someone to the airport or watering their plants while they're away."

"Is that on some list?"

"Maybe it should be." Eden Rose's smile was warm as pie.

The phone rang in the back room. Eden went to answer it, closing the door behind her. She had a strict policy against taking calls at the front counter, and to stymie any impulse to the contrary kept an old-fashioned, corded phone at her desk. Emet straightened some chairs. "Is that a good book?" he asked the little girl.

She nodded. "And the title is a joke, see? Because it's the *knight* at *dawn.*"

"That kind of joke is called a pun," said Emet. "Maybe you want to write it on the board."

The mother nodded, and the girl trotted over to the board where she copied the title in letters that started high on the left side of the board and tumbled down on the right like a waterfall. She put the chalk back in its holder and looked up at Emet.

"Good job," he said. "I like nice, big letters."

"Me, too," said the girl.

"I'll make you out a slip for a free refill," said Emet. "Your mom can keep it for you, and you can use it the next time you're here."

Eden Rose came out just as Emet was handing the girl her slip. She nodded at the back room and held open the door for him.

"What?" he said, walking past her as she closed the door.

"Strange phone call."

"About me?"

"Yes. I take it Bartholomew is your neighbor."

"He has the downstairs," said Emet.

"I always wondered where Bart lived. Anyway, he called to tell you that you had a visit from a November man with a foggy soul."

"I had a what from a what?"

"Loosely translated, someone tried to break into your apartment."

Emet laughed out loud. "Pickings must be pretty slim around here. The most expensive thing in there is my electric toothbrush."

"Bart says the man tried to plant drugs in your place."

"What?"

"Says he even showed him his wares."

"Oh, God." For the first time since Eden Rose had known him, Emet looked scared.

"Look, it's probably nothing," she began.

"You don't understand," said Emet. "My parole."

"Bart says he ran the guy off."

"What if he comes back? Or if he's been there before?"

"But—"

"If there's drugs in my place, they can put me back inside."

"Not without a trial."

"Yes without a trial. You don't know." He clenched his hands together. "My PO can come by my place any time he wants and look it over. He can call me here, he can call me at home. If I'm not where I'm supposed to be he can bust my chops. And if they find something—anything—they can send me back while they're investigating. They don't even need a warrant—they write their own."

"My God," said Eden Rose.

"Is Bart kidding? Tell me he was kidding."

"I'd trust Bart," said Eden Rose. She was untypically grave. "He likes the sound of his own voice, but he's no fool."

"Oh, God."

"So," said Eden, "what are you going to do?"

"I—don't know."

"Well, you'd better figure it out fast," said Eden Rose. "Bart said the guy asked for you by name."

"Jesus," said Emet. He looked around the small room and ran his fingers through his hair, accidentally pulling off his hair net. He crunched it in one hand. "I guess—I should call my parole officer. Not sure what else I can do."

"And Marty?"

"Yeah…."

"He's a good guy, Emet. And if you want to cover your ass—"

"I know." Emet reached into his back pocket to pull out his wallet. "How do you know Bart? Other than you know everybody."

"Everyone knows Bartholomew," said Eden Rose.

"Does he have a last name?" Emet opened his wallet and took out a business card. He sat at the desk and pulled the phone toward himself. "Mind?"

"Help yourself. No, he's kind of like Madonna and Cher that way."

"Oh."

"Bart the Bard, unofficial poet laureate of Oxbridge," said Eden Rose. "Does open mike nights all over town, and anyone can join in. Did one here a few months ago. When he left I found he'd written a poem on the wall in the ladies' loo—all about a woman whose soul was the color of water. Really beautiful."

"It's not there now." Emet often cleaned the bathrooms.

"Oh, I painted over it. I thought he should have asked permission first. But it was great, really spot-on."

Emet half-chuckled. Eden Rose went on, "He said you did him a favor of dubious repute not long ago."

"Oh—yeah. I broke into his apartment for him. He'd locked his keys inside." To Eden's arched eyebrow he said, "Hey, I didn't just learn cooking in there, you know." He lifted the receiver and dialed.

Eden closed the door and returned to the counter as a new customer walked in. His hair was gunmetal grey, and he would have been over six feet tall if he had not slouched. He wore khaki pants and a v-neck cashmere sweater over an Oxford shirt. His watch had been expensive many years ago, and his sneakers were stone-colored and supportive.

"Excuse me," he said to Ruthie. "I'm looking for the proprietor."

"That would be me," said Eden Rose. "How can I help you?"

He looked her up and down. "You're younger than I thought," he said.

The corner of Eden's mouth twitched. "It's a cross I have to bear," she said.

The man smiled sheepishly. "I'm sorry—many people look young to me these days." He held out his hand. "My name is Gene. I came in to apologize."

Eden Rose shook his hand. "Apologize for what?"

He withdrew his hand and pointed to the check taped to the front of the register. "That's mine."

"You didn't give me that," said Eden Rose.

"I know I didn't," said Gene. "But it's my check, and it's my own damn—" Eden coughed and glanced at the mother with the kids doing their homework. Gene flinched. "—darn fault it got stolen. I left my checkbook at a gas station when I went in to pay. Closed the account as soon as I realized what had happened, but yesterday I got a phone call from an officer, and he tells me some bum has been cashing checks in my good name all over town."

"I'd say it's the bum's fault," said Eden Rose. "But I appreciate your coming in."

"I'd like to make it up to you," said Gene. "Let me buy the amount he cheated you out of."

"That's very kind of you," she said, "but I'm not sure it's necessary."

"I'd be getting off easy here," he said. "I had to buy three gallons of antifreeze to square things at a garage outside of town."

"Oh, dear."

"And five pounds of bubble gum at a drug store. Fortunately, there are such things as grandchildren."

"It sounds like you've more than done your penance," said Eden. "No need to worry about a few cups of coffee here."

Gene glanced at the blackboard. "Young lady," he said, "you have forced my hand." He took a piece of chalk and wrote,

"Hush," he said, "the walls have ears." As indeed they did, since the landlord had atrocious taste in wallpaper.

"There," he said triumphantly. "But before I get my free refill, I have to buy a prefill. Am I correct?"

Eden Rose drew her brows together and pursed her lips. "Wordplay," she said finally. "I love it, but I'm not sure it counts as a pun."

"It says groaner."

"Rules are rules."

"Give me a moment," said Gene. He stared at the board and rubbed his chin with two fingers. His eyes lit up. Seizing a piece of chalk he wrote,

Daniel Boone knew the backwoods. Indeed, it is said he knew them backwoods and forewoods.

"Hah!" said Gene.

Eden Rose smiled. "Out-maneuvered on my own territory. What can I get you? The flavor of the day is Hazelnut Pumpkin Spice."

"Hold on a moment," said Gene severely. "You know as well as I do that a cup of coffee won't cover that check." He glanced at the study group. "What if you let me get something for the kids over there?"

"You'll have to check with their mother first," said Eden Rose.

"That's so sweet," said the mother. "Just this once."

"Yaay!" shouted the boy. "This time *you* can have the muffin, and *I* can have the morning bun!"

"That's genius!" shouted the girl.

"Inside voices," said the mother. Ruthie plated a muffin and a morning bun and walked over to the table with them.

"Why don't you sit there, and I'll bring your coffee?" suggested Eden Rose. She led Gene to a table and filled his mug. Ruthie whisked the carafe from Eden Rose's hand and replaced it at the counter.

"Join me?" said Gene. "My wife's very understanding about such things. She's French."

Ruthie gave Eden Rose a smile and a confident nod, and Eden sat. "I can take a break for a minute or two."

Gene took a sip of coffee. "This is very good," he said.

“Thanks. We roast our own.”

“A lot of places over-roast it.” He took another sip. “The best coffee I ever had was when I was stationed in Vienna. But this runs a close second, and that’s saying something.”

“I’ll take it as a compliment,” she said. “Were you in the military?”

“Korea.”

“So was my father,” she said.

“Was he? Where did he serve?”

“He missed the action. The war ended while he was still in basic training.”

“Ah.”

“But not you, sounds like.”

“My timing wasn’t as good, no.”

“You must have started before he did.”

“At Fort Devens,” he said. “But it can’t have been much earlier. The war ended a few months after I reached it, which was certainly a relief, though we always had the sense that the brass weren’t really sure what to do with a peacetime army. So like a lot of the boys, I went any number of places after that.”

“My dad talked a lot about his Army time. I think it changed him.”

“It changed us all.” Gene took another sip. “The entire country.”

"How so?"

Gene chuckled. "Universal draft. Now there was a transformation, if you please."

"Because?"

"Try this on for size," said Gene. "Imagine meeting people you'd heard of but never seen in real life—and suddenly you're all dressed the same and eating the same rotten food and gearing up to fight someone else's war thousands of miles away. I wouldn't have signed up for that in a million years."

"I can see why not," said Eden Rose.

"But there I was anyway, thanks to my local draft board. And it was a whole new world." He set his mug down. "The kaleidoscopic human variety of America was something I experienced for the first time in the Army. Why, I'd never heard an actual Southern accent before then, believe it or not."

"Really?"

"I lived near Blue Hill Avenue, south of Boston. Plenty of stores still had signs in Yiddish and Hebrew. Everyone called it Jew Hill Avenue. "

"No one would say that now."

"Back then we did. And there were no blacks south of the Franklin Park Zoo, none." He took another sip, savoring it. "Then—the Army. Talk about culture shock."

"I can imagine."

"Can you?"

"Sure. A Hollywood World War II bomber crew, you know? One guy named Tex, one blonde kid from the Midwest—"

"—and one federally mandated tough-talker from the Bronx," said Gene. "But that World War II bomber crew was all white."

"True."

"Korea wasn't like that." Gene seemed to have forgotten his coffee. He leaned forward, eyes intense. "One day you're home surrounded by people who all look like you and talk like you and pray like you, and that's what's normal. Then your induction notice arrives. Suddenly you're thousands of miles away, depending for your life on men your parents wouldn't have let your sister marry a few weeks before. Talk about change! And it didn't stop after the war, either. Do you really think the Civil Rights Movement would have happened without the integration of the military?"

"I never thought about it."

"Young men who have risked their lives in battle for their country prefer not to sit at the back of the bus."

"Bet they liked to be served at lunch counters too."

"And vote," agreed Gene. "We seemed to have the wherewithal to make things happen back then." He picked up his mug once more. "Once Truman signed that order, if you were in the military you were going to meet people you would never meet anywhere else. You might not want to be there—I certainly didn't—but once you were in, everyone was treated the same way. You might say equally badly, but equally. There's nowhere else I can think of where that's true."

"I see what you mean," said Eden Rose.

"My unit was integrated," went on Gene. "Meaning we had one black man. Everyone was always very polite to him, to prove they weren't racist."

Eden lifted a small smile. "Did he notice?"

"Since he wasn't an idiot, yes. His name was Sammy, and he was from Roxbury. Near Boston," he explained to her puzzled expression. "Meanest, baddest part of town—at least it was then. Probably three miles from my house, but Sammy and I never would have met except for the Army. And all those polite people in our unit were scared to death of him."

"Oh, lordy."

"He was all right, though."

"How so?"

"Well." Gene paused. "I don't want to bore you with all this."

"Far from it," said Eden Rose. "This reminds me of my dad's stories. Please go on."

Gene took another sip and put his mug down. "Would you like to hear a tale from my decadent youth?"

"Absolutely."

"Because I warn you, I was not always the clean-living specimen you see before you." Gene's voice slowed and deepened, taking on a storyteller's cadences. "In fact, on one occasion when Sammy and I were stationed together at Fort Devens, I had a forty-eight-hour pass, and I took the opportunity to go into Boston and get completely blotto."

"Gracious," said Eden Rose, as if she could not imagine such a thing.

"In fact, young lady, I was so completely spiflicated that I apparently suffered a lapse of judgment—or several—and went into a section of town that was best left to its own devices, at least if you happened to be an extremely unsober young man with a full wallet and delusions of immortality. I have a vague recollection of being surrounded by some unfriendly locals who took exception to me." He shook his head. "I woke up the next morning battered but sober, and denuded of both my delusions and my wallet. I made it back to Fort Devens with eight minutes left on my pass, thanks to a taxi driver who took pity on a desperate soldier. He had been in the previous war, so he told me, and he had some sympathy." Gene chuckled and shook his head.

"As soon as I walked into the barracks," he went on, "Sammy took one look at me and said," Gene glanced at the table with the young children and lowered his voice, "'What in the *hell* happened to you?' So I told him. And he hopped out of his bunk and his eyes narrowed—I tell you, like knives—and he said, 'Where was you?' And I said," here Gene assumed a bleary expression, as one who knows mainly that he was severely drunk the night before, "'It was thus-and-such a place.' But Sammy wouldn't let it go. 'What corner was it? You sure?' And then he left."

"Left where?" said Eden Rose.

"Walked off the base."

"Was he allowed to do that?"

"Of course not. But the MPs were scared of him."

Eden laughed.

"Everyone was," said Gene. "Anyway, that night he strolled back, tossed me my wallet with all the cash and the checkbook in it, and said, 'Here. Next time don't be so damn stupid.'"

"No."

"Yes."

Eden Rose shook her head. "That's amazing."

"And do you know," said Gene, "that that was the only other time I ever lost my checkbook?"

"Maybe you could call Sammy," said Eden Rose.

"I wish I could," said Gene. "He died in Korea."

"How awful," said Eden Rose.

Gene sighed. "I only feel old when I find myself saying, 'Those were the good old days.' But I just don't see that kind of heroism any more, the kind you used to find in ordinary people."

"Human nature hasn't changed," said Eden Rose.

"No," he said, "but I think our expectations have." His smile was melancholy as he raised his mug. Eden Rose hoisted an invisible one.

"To Sammy, wherever he is," said Gene. "A man of his time. They don't make 'em like that any more."

Eden Rose tipped her fist towards Gene's mug. "Clink," she said.

15

Mercey talked to Serena constantly. During training sessions for the dog handlers, the teacher had impressed upon the class the importance of engaging the dogs. "Tell 'em good morning, kiss 'em good night, ask 'em what color socks you should wear today," he said. Their future owners would talk to them, he said, commands and corrections and requests for help of all kinds. The dogs needed to learn to listen. Mercey had taken the directive to heart, and now she kept up a stream of chatter with her dog that would have put Johnny Quest and Bandit to shame. Right now she was packing and trying to convince Serena that the hand-held tape dispenser was not a menace to all things canine.

"Look," she urged, kneeling next to a box. She held the flaps down and placed the tape dispenser on the seam. "Come on, girl."

Serena drew closer, peering at the box. As Mercey drew the tape across the seam, the dispenser screeched. Serena leaped backwards like an Alsatian crawdad, hind legs scrambling under her belly.

"It's not going to hurt you," said Mercey. She held out the dispenser and Serena advanced, neck stretched to the fullest, and sniffed. But as soon as Mercey taped another box with it and the screeching recommenced, Serena hurtled away again. She barked at it. The dispenser did not bark back. This went on for half an hour, whereupon Serena, perhaps finding that constant vigilance was thirsty work, trotted downstairs to her water bowl. Mercey filled another box and pushed the flaps together.

Serena came back to the room. She whined, turning in tight circles.

"Wussup, babe?" said Mercey.

Serena whined again. Mercey abandoned the packing and followed her dog down to the kitchen. Serena led her to her food and water bowls and stared at them.

"What?" said Mercey.

Serena looked at Mercey, her brown eyes peaking in anxiety.

"What?" repeated Mercey. "You're not being clear at all."

Serena took a half step toward the water bowl and whined some more.

"You can't be thirsty," said Mercedes. "There's plenty in there." She knelt and tilted the bowl. "See?"

Serena approached, her front paws jumpy on the lichen-green linoleum. She lapped up a tongueful of water, then snorted in disgust and backed away, her tongue flapping over her white teeth.

"Serena?" said Mercedes. She looked from the unhappy dog to the water dish. Confusion and betrayal filled Serena's liquid brown eyes.

Mercedes paused, then dipped a finger into the bowl. "I can't believe I'm doing this," she muttered, and licked it.

She spat.

Mercey poured the water into the sink. She took a mixing bowl from the cabinet and filled it. As fresh water ran into the clean bowl, she rinsed her mouth and spat again. She set the fresh bowl before Serena, who gulped it in great relief.

"At least it was only salt," she told the dog. "This time. I hope." She clenched her hands. "Fucking *hell.*"

Serena lifted her wet muzzle from the bowl and waved her tail reassuringly. She walked over and leaned her full eighty pounds against Mercey, lifting her head to be petted as she mashed the woman against the wall. Mercey scratched behind the dog's ears. "We have to get you somewhere safe."

They darted upstairs. Mercey reached into her purse, still talking to the dog. "We'll move in a day early, and I can come back tomorrow to finish packing." She pulled her hand out and squinted into the little bag, then groped again. Finally, she emptied it onto her bed.

No phone.

The house did not have a landline. Mercedes had cancelled it when Clay's friends started leaving messages for him about drug purchases. The account was in her name, and she had no interest in finding out if this made her an accessory to narcotics trafficking.

The house was a strange, empty shell with no way to call out.

Mercey shoved everything back into her purse and slung it over one shoulder so the long strap hung across her chest. She pulled on a windbreaker and yanked the hood over her head. Squatting, she slipped a blue NEADS vest onto Serena's shoulders, and clicked the leash onto the dog's collar. They walked to the head of the stairs. At a hand signal from Mercey, Serena sat. Mercey waited. No sound came from the cellar. She made a second hand signal, and Serena walked beside her down the stairs, matching her pace and keeping the lead slack.

Mercey opened the door. The sky was dark and morose, and drizzle slithered in the air. Water slicked the sidewalks with copper-colored puddles, and the streets were full of diseased rainbows where cars had dripped their fluids.

They flew down the street. Serena bounded by Mercey's side, her paws thumping on the sidewalk with a sound like a heartbeat.

It was nearly noon when Mercedes and Serena tumbled through the open door of the Serve You Right Café. Mercey's cheeks were cardinal-red, and she was breathing hard. Serena gave an exuberant snort and shook herself, flinging mist onto the chairs and tables.

"Can I help you?" said Eden Rose, her secret equilibrium still firmly in place.

Mercey looked around the café, still gasping. The only customer was Gene, who was nursing his second cup of Hazelnut Pumpkin Spice. He smiled at Serena as he wiped the dogspray off his table with a paper napkin. "Is Emet First here?" she said finally.

Emet emerged from the back room, where he had just finished phoning the parole office and talking to Marty the cop. "Mercey?"

"I'm so sorry to bother you at work." Her voice quaked at the edges.

“What’s wrong?” Emet strode around the counter and pulled out a chair.

Mercey sat down. “He took my phone,” she said. Her voice cracked. “And there’s no landline, so I couldn’t call anyone—and I knew you’d be here—and he was hurting Serena—” Her face crumpled.

“Who?”

“My brother.” She drew a shuddering breath. “He thinks—well, never mind what he thinks—but he put salt in her water and if her training program ever finds out she’s been abused they’ll take her away from me—”

Eden Rose set a bowl of water on the floor and a plate of dog biscuits on the table. Serena lapped at the bowl and lifted her head to peer at the treats, keeping her dripping muzzle a molecule away from the edge of the table. Mercey handed her a biscuit, and the dog lipped it away from her before downing it in a single crunch. She sat and fixed the rest of the biscuits with a deep, brown stare, daring them to make a false move.

“Appetite’s good,” said Emet.

“And she ran all the way over here,” admitted Mercey. She rested her hand on the dog’s head. The tips of her fingers wobbled.

“You can take her to the vet if you’re worried.”

"He took my phone. He wrecked my car. I couldn't call, I couldn't take her to the hospital."

"There's a phone in the back room," said Eden Rose. "Help yourself."

"Thank you," whispered Mercey. Her face grew red again, and she blinked.

"More to the point," said Emet, "how are *you?*"

Mercedes gave a stifled shriek of laughter. "Oh, I'm fine. I'm not the one he tried to poison."

"Your brother."

"Oh, God." She put her face in her hands. "I'm so ashamed."

"Why?"

She put her hands down. "This is my family. This is what they're like." She wiped under her sodden eyes with the ball of her thumb.

Emet handed her a paper napkin. "You can't blame yourself for what your family is like."

"Sure I can," she muttered, dabbing her eyes.

"Not if it makes you cry like this," he said.

"Never stopped me before."

"But you'll get dehydrated."

Mercey gave a damp hiccup that might have been a laugh. Emet smiled. A new song started, and Jim Morrison assured his lady that he was gonna love her till the heavens stopped the rain and various other celestial and atmospheric phenomena occurred. Emet perked up. "The breakfast song!" he exclaimed.

"What?"

Emet deepened his voice and sang along with the tune. "Come on, come on, come on, now crunchy flakes! Can't you see? I'm going to be late. What are these waffles that you made? I don't need no scrambled eggs!"

Mercedes giggled. "Okay," she said. "I think I can make that phone call now." She followed Emet into the back room and dialed the vet, who happily had an appointment available in an hour. Serena followed them, snuffling at Emet in joyful approval.

As they returned to the table, Gene rose and joined them. "Excuse me," he said to Mercey. "I don't mean to intrude, but I have a debt of honor to pay here, and I wondered if you would let me buy you a cup of coffee."

"Ah…."

"Go ahead," said Emet. "He's been buying drinks for the house all morning."

"It's a long story," said Gene, "but I have a few dollars left to clear my name, and I'd consider it money well spent if you'd let me buy you a drink with no ulterior motive attached or implied."

Mercey smiled. "Well, in that case," she said, "thanks."

"What kind?" called Eden Rose from behind the counter as Ruthie selected a clean mug.

Gene appraised Mercedes. "I may be a sexist old man, but I have noticed over the years that young ladies are very fond of chocolate, especially in times of stress. So I'm going to suppose either a hot cocoa or a mocha with whipped cream."

"Wow," said Mercey. "It's like you're a psychic, beverage-dispensing Santa Claus."

"Mocha, then?"

"Please. But no caffeine."

"Decaf mocha with whipped cream," said Gene.

"I'll do it," said Emet, and walked behind the counter.

Gene sat down and reached for a biscuit. "May I?"

"Sure."

He gave it to Serena, who shattered it with one bite and swallowed the pieces. He waited till she was done, then stroked her ears. "She's beautiful. Service dog?"

"In training."

"Hullo, pup." Once again, Gene's voice softened. He smiled into Serena's brown eyes. "I had a dog like this, many years ago."

"They're great," said Mercey.

Gene slipped his fingers under the dog's ears and rubbed in little circles. His hands were patched the color of café au lait, and his veins stood out. He looked at Serena as though he could not get enough. "His name was Hunter. Bigger than this lovely lady, but otherwise they could be twins. He belonged to my friend Sammy when we were stationed in Korea. Saved his life more times than either of us cared to think."

"I thought you said he was your dog."

"Not at first. He and Sammy were a team."

"So how did he come to be yours?"

Gene sighed. "Hunter was injured—it was so banal, really. He cut his pad on a piece of broken glass on the base. So that one night, Sammy had to go out without him. He never came back. Sniper."

"I'm so sorry," said Mercey. And she was.

"It was a long time ago," said Gene gently. "But Hunter was a good dog and he had been Sammy's dog, so I asked if I could have him and the brass said yes. After the war ended, I had him shipped to my sister in the States. I used to send her a dollar a week so she could take him out for ice cream. He had certainly earned it. And every week she would send me a thank-you note from him."

"No. Really?"

"It turned out Hunter had an unexpected literary streak."

"Do you still have them?"

"Every one. I thought as soon as I was discharged that Hunter and I could get a bachelor pad together. I had all sorts of plans for how he was going to help me in my dating life—I believe the term is 'chick magnet'? And Hunter had a charisma that ought not to have been legal. Girls adored him. But then I met a young lady in Paris, and *Ooh la la!"*

Somewhere in the depths of Gene's voice was another café where a chanteuse sang through azure tobacco smoke, and outside in a long-ago street a small boy ran past wearing short pants and carrying a loaf of bread as long as he was tall. "So I asked her if she liked dogs. She said yes, so I got down on bended knee, and God bless her, she said yes again. When my tour of duty was over we came back to the States. I picked up Hunter, and he lived with me and my wife and then our kids for many years."

Behind the counter, air and sweet liquid hissed into mug. Emet reached for whipped cream and spices.

"That's a beautiful story," said Mercey.

Gene went on, lost to the present. "One night he woke up screaming," he said. "I took him to the emergency room at the vet's. It was renal failure. The doctor said, 'I can keep him alive, but you won't be doing him any favors.' I said, 'He saved my life and God knows how many other men's. Do what's best for him.' So the doctor put him down and I left. It was just about dawn then. I found the highest hill I could climb and cried all day."

Mercedes looked at Gene with tear-shattered eyes. She rubbed a magical spot on Serena's jaw. The dog lifted her head and pressed toward Mercey's hand.

"I know a man's not supposed to cry," said Gene, pulling his hands back to his lap.

Classic rock played over the speakers. A college couple came in, walking in step while staring at their cell phones and thumbing the keypads. Gene glanced at the counter. "Your drink is ready," he said, and, smiling, walked to the counter to pay.

Emet put the mocha in front of Mercedes and sat. “Feel any better?”

She took a sip and put the mug down. “I feel like an idiot.”

“So that would be better?” he said hopefully.

“I’m so sorry.”

“Don’t apologize.”

“I’m bothering you at work.”

“Slow day.”

“My family’s so Godawful, Emet. You have no idea.”

“I bet I do.”

“There’s nobody I could introduce you to if you wanted to meet them.”

“Okay.”

“And I suck at relationships.”

Emet chuckled darkly. “Me too. You could say.”

Mercey half-smiled. “Okay. You might have the edge on me there.”

“Score.”

“It’s just…” she trailed off.

"What?"

She sighed. "I have this stupid, stupid idea…I keep thinking that if I hang in there long enough they'll come around."

"Mm."

"It's not working out too good."

"Everybody has a crazy family."

She took another sip. "What's yours like?"

Emet rubbed his knuckles. "I don't have much in the way of relatives," he said.

"No?"

"There's my mom. In Boston."

"Mine's local." She wrinkled her nose.

"Does it matter?"

Mercey put her cup down. "It shouldn't."

"But it does."

"Yes."

Emet brightened. "Hold on a sec—think I might have something." He glanced at Eden Rose.

"Oh, my, look at the time," said Eden Rose. "Take fifteen, Emet."

Emet gave a shy grin. He slipped into the back room, one hand pulling off his hair net and the other yanking his apron string. He emerged a moment later, zipping up his windbreaker. "Ready?" he said.

Mercey stood. "Where are we going?"

"I have magical grandparents."

They walked across the street, Serena padding at Mercey's side. The sun was not yet visible, but the clouds glowed white, and in the park the puddles shone like coins scattered in a busker's hat. By the fountain, Isadore and Daisy were doing close-up magic for a group of college students who were trying to figure out the trick. Isadore had just burned a card to ashes, then removed it, unscathed, from a young man's hat. "Do it again," said one of the students.

"Not on your life, son," replied Isadore.

As Emet and Mercey joined the small crowd, Daisy's mint-green eyes lit up. She pushed her way toward them, beaming.

"You must be the young lady Emet was telling us about," she said. "I had *so* been hoping we would meet you."

After Emet and Mercey came back from the park, Eden Rose lent Mercedes her car to take Serena to the animal clinic. They put a spare apron across the back seat for the dog to lie on, and Mercey drove to the office, admonishing Serena not to shed along the way. Eden Rose and Emet waved from the window of the café.

"Lovely young woman," said Eden Rose.

"Yeah." Emet watched the car. "What the hell does she see in me?"

"Now, there's a puzzler. Why don't you ask her?"

"If I see her again."

"Why wouldn't you?"

"Hard to have a second date if they revoke my parole."

"They can't do that!"

"I called the office," said Emet. "Talked to the on-call officer. Know what she said?"

"What?"

Emet grimaced. "She goes, 'Nice try, First. If you don't know this guy, how is it he's asking for you by name?'"

"What did she mean, 'Nice try'?"

"She thinks I'm covering for something."

"By telling them about it?"

"So when I get caught they go easy on me."

"But you've never done drugs. Why would she think you'd start now?"

Emet sighed and looked out the window. "I knew a guy once," he said. "He was walking home from work and he sees a crowd and a bunch of cruisers with lights flashing. So he goes over, and it's in front of the public library and the lawn is cordoned off with crime scene tape. So he's like, 'What's going on?' and a cop says there's a body, looks like a homicide. And the guy looks, and it's his wife there on the ground."

Eden Rose flinched.

"So he's screaming her name. '*Michelle! Michelle!*' And he starts running toward her. And the cop at the perimeter yells, 'Tackle!' and three of them jump him and bring him down."

"Dear God. Why?"

"So he wouldn't contaminate the crime scene."

"Oh—my lord. That poor man."

"You'd think so." Emet turned to look at Eden Rose. "Thing is, he really was the one that killed her. He was trying to drop a bunch of his DNA and prints there so when the DA presents it as evidence against him, the defense attorneys say, 'Of course that's his DNA. We have multiple witnesses that saw him running all over the crime scene after the fact.'"

Eden Rose closed her eyes and shook her head.

"So the on-call PO says she's gonna call my guy and they'll have a case conference with his supervisor." Emet shoved his hands into his pockets. "And they need some more of my pee, so I gotta take part of the afternoon off. Sorry."

"They can't come here?"

"Pee is more special when they collect it at the Community Corrections Center."

Eden Rose sighed. "Well, don't worry about the time off, anyway."

"Thanks, boss lady."

"Emet," said Eden Rose. "I can tell them you're here all day every day you're scheduled. I'll tell them I've never seen any evidence of drugs or anything else."

"Marty said pretty much the same thing," said Emet. "Thanks. They'll probably be calling."

"And you called them right away. That should count for something."

"Yeah, well, I have to tell them whenever I talk to any cops."

"Why?"

"Any law enforcement contact."

"I didn't know that."

"Now you know."

"What did Marty say?"

For the first time, Emet smiled. "I felt like he believed me."

"He probably did."

"He said it was likely a case of mistaken identity because Western Mass has a serious drug problem and they were probably looking for someone else. He said if it was a frame-up, it was the lamest one he'd ever heard of, and anyway framing someone in real life is harder than in the movies. And then he went to talk to Bart."

"Could he tell the parole office that?"

"He said he would." Emet turned back to the window, frowning in the direction Eden Rose's car had gone. "I need to find out who's doing this."

"You will."

"I better." Emet spoke under his breath so softly his words blended with the hum of the coffee shop. "Because I am never, ever going back in there."

Mercedes and Serena sat in a small examining room. Posters showing different kinds of ferrets and pet rabbits adorned the walls, and the floor smelled of antiseptic. The door opened and Dr. Roch came in. She was a motherly type with frizzy grey hair growing out of an auburn dye job. Her eyes crinkled like raisins, and she lifted her chin so Serena could lick it. "So what do we have here?"

Mercedes told her what had happened.

"Did she drink much of it?" said Dr. Roch.

"Probably none. She just kept whining and making faces."

"If she spat it out, there's no problem."

"Her appetite's good, and so's her energy."

"Good. Well, salt will show up in her kidneys, so we'll do a CBC. Meanwhile, let's check out the rest of her."

The doctor inspected the dog's heartbeat (normal) and temperature, which Serena endured with wounded dignity. She took a vial of blood while Mercey held Serena's collar and murmured to her that she was a good girl.

"This will take about forty-five minutes," said the vet.

"Mind if I wait?"

"I'll need this room, but you can take a seat in the waiting area."

Mercey and Serena left the room, and the vet strode out to the back of the clinic and handed the dark red vial to a tech in scrubs. "CBC," she said, and the young woman nodded and took it away. The doctor sat down at her desk and picked up the phone, dialing a number she knew by heart.

"Chief Brunette here, and why are you bothering me at home?" said a voice.

Mark Brunette was the head of the MSPCA's Law Enforcement Team. Every vet in the state had his home and cell numbers in case any of the local animal abusers failed to stick to a nine-to-five weekday schedule.

"Hi, Chief. Nichola Roch. Sorry to bother you. Animal cruelty case."

"I didn't think it was a social call." He sighed. "Is this weekend bad or wait till Monday bad?"

"Not sure yet. We're waiting on a CBC." She sketched in the details.

"How's the dog?" said the chief.

"Seemed perky enough."

"If it's an emergency, I can scare up the manpower to start the investigation today," said the chief. "Otherwise we're talking Monday at the earliest."

"I hate the idea of waiting," said Dr. Roch.

"Is the animal suffering?"

"If I say yes, can you get things going today?"

"Just the facts, ma'am."

Dr Roch drummed on the desk with a pen. The tip landed in a dark mess of pockmarks where she had tapped many times before. "She's not in any obvious distress, but we don't have the lab results in yet."

"And the brother hasn't done this before?"

"Not as far as the owner knows, no."

"Hate to let you down, doc, but I think this is one for the back burner," said the chief. "Email me everyone's contact info, and I'll be on it first thing Monday. And tell the owner to keep her dog away from the abuser."

"I'd really like to nip this one in the bud before he gets creative."

"Can't say I blame you. We'll be in touch with the owner soon as we can."

"And the brother?"

"Did she see him hurt the dog?"

"She's sure he was the culprit. They're the only two in the house, and she says there haven't been any visitors."

"The animal's not suffering, it's not an emergency."

"I know."

"If it is, I can maybe send someone over."

"I know."

"Otherwise, I just don't have the staffing."

"Let me think." The pen rapped on the desktop in a staccato burst. "Chief. Do you remember that case last year when that kid was abusing the family cat and he ended up assaulting his mother?"

"Any similarities to this case?"

"How many do you need?"

"Whatcha got?"

Dr. Roch put down the battle-weary pen and rubbed her chin with one finger. "He's been verbally abusive to his sister. He's committed property crimes and petty theft against her. It looks like an escalating pattern to me. And he's a known drug user."

"That's something," said the chief. "He might be a danger to the community."

"He might."

She waited.

"We have a trainee on staff," said Brunette finally. "Might be good for her to get a taste of an emergency investigation."

"Thanks, Chief."

"What we're here for."

"Normal," said the vet.

Mercey heaved an enormous sigh. "Thank God." She looked at Serena. "Had me scared there, babe."

"I've reported the incident to the MSPCA," said the doctor.

"Will they need to talk to me?"

"Yes."

Mercey took out her card. "They can call me at work."

The vet slipped the card into her pocket. "Have you told the NEADS people?"

"I will."

"If someone's trying to hurt her, you need to keep her out of that situation."

"Don't worry," said Mercey. "There's no way I'm taking her back there."

"Do you have a place to stay?"

"I'll figure something out."

"Do you have a place to stay?" said Emet. They were back at the Serve You Right Café, and Mercey was helping him wipe down tables. Serena was dozing in a corner, and the Closed sign hung on the door. Eden Rose was removing the day's pastries from the display case and boxing them up. A volunteer from the

Oxbridge food pantry came for them every other day after the close of business.

"No," admitted Mercey. "I called my girlfriend's home phone, but she's not answering and I don't know her cell number. My other friend has allergies so she won't take Serena. I'll find something."

"Does your brother know who your friends are?" said Eden Rose.

"Yes."

"Then you might not be safe with any of them tonight," said Eden Rose.

Mercey sighed. Serena lifted her head, wagged her tail, and returned to the serious business of napping.

"I'd offer my place," said Emet, "but, um, I'm really not set up for company." A blush darkened his cheekbones.

Mercey beamed at him in utter enchantment. "You are so *gallant*. Did you know that?"

"Rumors," said Emet.

"Stay with me," said Eden Rose. "I'm close. Two cats, no allergies. We can maybe reach your friend on Facebook, and you can leave Serena with me while you finish moving."

"Oh, no," said Mercey. "I can't ask you to do that."

"You're not. I'm offering. And unlike *certain* people," she glared at Emet, "I have a sofa bed."

Mercey giggled. Emet ducked his head and swabbed furiously at a clean table. “Man,” he muttered, “chicks are mean.”

The knocking at the door was insistent, and interspersed with blasts on the buzzer. Clay lumbered up the stairs, scowling. It was 5:00, not the usual time for the mail or UPS, and anyway they never knocked. He had been online, conferring with his friends about how best to address the situation with his sister and Emet; but the party or parties at the door were clearly not to be deterred. "Fucking Jehovah's Witnesses," he muttered. "Jesus saves, but not when the Fed cuts the interest rates." He flung open the door. "What?"

A man and a woman stood on the steps. Her hair was dark red and braided; his was buzzed down to the scalp. They wore matching uniforms, tan slacks and dark green shirts with tan epaulets and pocket tabs of the same color. Holsters and handcuffs hung from their belts, and the man wore a brass badge over his left breast pocket.

Clay's hand froze on the doorknob.

"Mr. Finch?" said the man. The words and the tone were polite, but his face was hard. Next to him, the woman stood tall and professionally straight.

"You're not cops," said Clay.

"We're with the Massachusetts Society for the Prevention of Cruelty to Animals," said the man. "We're investigating a report of—"

Clay burst out laughing. "Dog cops," he roared. "Holy *shit.*"

The woman spoke for the first time. "Are you Clayton Finch?"

"Maybe," said Clay. He was still laughing. "I'll see if he's home."

"Mr. Finch, we're investigating a report of animal cruelty," said the woman.

"There's no dog here," said Clay. He pushed open the door with his foot, showing the foyer and part of the living room.

"What makes you think the report was about a dog?" said the man.

Clay shrugged elaborately.

"Our information says that an animal at this address was being abused," said the woman. "Someone was salting its drinking water."

Clay chuckled. "What happens if you haul someone downtown?" he said. "Lock 'em in the doghouse?"

The man's face kept its hard look. "If the report is true, and if it happens again and the animal is injured, the perpetrator could face criminal charges."

Clay threw up his hands and shook them in a Bob Fosse parody. "Ooh, I'm so scared of the dog cops and their fancy uniforms. What do you do to the bad guys—take away their squeaky toys? Make them eat dry instead of canned?"

"Mr. Finch," said the man.

"Who sent you?" said Clay. "My sister? Or that freak she's dating?"

"Animal abuse is a felony in Massachusetts," said the woman.

"Bullshit," said Clay.

"And we can serve warrants, make arrests, and testify in criminal cases," said the woman. Her hand rested on her belt, near the cuffs. "But we'd prefer to talk to you about the situation with the dog."

"Dream on," said Clay.

The man spoke. "Our only concern is the animal's well-being, Mr. Finch. Can we come in and discuss this?"

"Got a warrant?" said Clay.

"No," said the man.

"Not yet," said the woman at the same time.

"Then shut up and leave me alone." Clay stepped back and started to pull the door closed.

"Mr. Finch—" began the woman.

Clay yanked open the door. "I told you," he screamed, "I'm not home!" He slammed the door. The sound of his footfalls thudded through the wall and faded.

The man looked at the door. He ran his hands over his short hair and sighed. The woman turned to him. "Does it always go that well?" she said.

Clay ran out the back door, dialing on Mercey's phone.

"Adam," he hissed when the call went through, "you will not fucking believe this, man. The bitch turned me in."

"No way, dude." Adam laughed. "That is harsh."

"Cops, man. I am serious. They came to my door. I barely got away."

"Why would Mercey turn you in?" said Adam. "She never cared about your deviant life choices before."

"Not about the—" Clay dropped his voice. "Not about the weed, man. This was about that bitch of hers."

"Why? What you do to the dog?"

"Who cares, man? The point is she set me up."

"The dog or your sister?"

"Don't be a fucking—moron." Clay was gasping. "Thing is, I don't know if it was Mercey—or that creep she's banging. Or maybe that guy—at his place—this morning. Someone!"

"Hey, Clay-man," said Adam. "If Mercey had a rat instead of a dog, do you think they'd be trying to nail you on Mickey Mouse charges?"

The cataract of vitriol Clay spewed into the phone was broken only by Adam's hazy laughter whenever Clay paused for a breath. He stopped at a street corner, panting into the phone, knees shaking. He had run half a block.

"I can't breathe," he gasped. His hand gripped his shirt and twisted it over his chest. "That bastard is killing me."

Adam was still laughing. "Dude, you get winded reaching for a beer."

Clay heaved a breath, and another. "I'm—not—laughing. This is serious. That sack of shit is going to ruin my life."

"Only if you let him, my man." Adam's voice was tinny over the small speaker in the cell phone. "I am not one to tell you how to live your life. But you gotta do something to get back in control."

Clay choked down another breath. "Everything—was fine—till he showed up."

"There's your problem," said Adam. "And there's your solution."

"What?"

Adam's voice turned serious. "Your sister's dating an ex-con, man. That is not healthy. And he is trying to screw you. It's simple math, Clay. One minus one. Stop him before he destroys you."

Clay drew in as much air as he could. "I will," he said. "I will."

Mercey insisted on taking Eden Rose out to dinner as a thank-you, so it was late when they walked into the apartment. The cats took one look at Serena and flickered away to their secret cat places. Serena took one look at the cats' food and plunged into it with dolphin-like élan, her muzzle half-buried in the fishy-smelling nuggets. Delicate negotiations ensued: Mercey held onto the dog's collar and Eden Rose whisked the dishes onto the kitchen counter. Squirming and whining, Serena pointed out that possession was nine-tenths of the law, and the cats' absence signaled their relinquishment of their food to any such party or parties who happened to be nearby and hungry. Mercey rebutted, noting that she and Serena were guests, and Serena could eat the kibble she, Mercey, had picked up at the convenience store. As Serena's opinion was distinctly in the minority, she ultimately acquiesced, gulping down her meal while keeping one eye on the counter as Eden Rose topped off the cats' dishes.

Eden Rose propped open the door to the bathroom with a heavy doorstop so the cats could get to the kitty litter box but

Serena couldn't. The animals being settled, Eden pulled the sofa bed open—it filled two-thirds of the living room—and got bedclothes from the linen closet. They smelled of lavender and almond. She and Mercey set to making the bed, their hands working in tandem. Darkness pressed against the windows, but inside the small apartment, table lamps and an overhead light in the kitchen held the silky-black night at bay.

"This is so nice of you." Mercedes squatted to yank a corner of the fitted sheet over the mattress. "I don't know what I would have done."

"You'd have found someone."

"Or spent the night in a storm drain under the highway."

"You know, that sounds like so much fun," said Eden Rose. "But I bet there's a downside."

"Beats going home," said Mercey.

"You must know people in the area."

"Growing up, I spent a lot of time taking care of my mom," said Mercey. "I mean, I have a few friends, but without my cell—I hardly know any phone numbers any more."

"I know what you mean," said Eden Rose.

"And my grad school friends are all in New Haven and stuff, so." Mercey straightened up. Her voice was full of untold story.

"Is your mom ill?"

Eden's tone was quiet and receptive, inviting confidences without demanding them.

"My whole family is sick," said Mercey. And her tale came pouring out.

Mercedes Finch was the brood hen of her family. When her mother's multiple sclerosis had first appeared many years before, Mercedes had learned everything she could about the disease to take care of her. (The list of salient facts—it was a degenerative, life-shortening, neurological disease with no known cure—was depressingly short.) When her father abandoned the family for a younger, sexier woman who was not confined to a wheelchair, Mercey spread her wings over her mother and her brother, working two jobs after school to stock the kitchen with store-brand Cheerios, day-old bread, and milk. She consulted with her local pharmacist and got generic meds for her mother's bathroom cabinet. She found state-sponsored programs that would supply some nursing care at home. When her mother used the illness as an excuse to let her natural bitterness flow unabated, Clay retreated to the basement in a haze of pot smoke and Mercey went to college on a scholarship.

In high school and later in college, Mercey saw that when she talked to other people the way her family talked, she was abrasive and off-putting; and the people she liked did not like her. So she studied the popular girls—not mean-popular, but nice-popular—to crack their system. She saw that whenever they said "Thanks," they made eye contact. That if they gave a compliment, which was often, what they said was true. That unlike her family, they did not litter their conversation with casual curses; and that when meeting someone for the first time they did not interrogate but conversed, so the new person felt safe. Mercey copied their ways, making them hers even as she earned a bachelor of science, then placed into a program that granted her a master's and a doctorate of physical therapy.

"Sounds like you're the white sheep of your family," said Eden Rose.

"I told Emet some of it," she said. "I never know when to bring this garbage up. If I do it too early I feel like the guy will bolt. If I do it too late I feel like a liar."

"So what do you do?"

"Usually I just act weird and neurotic till I drive the dude away."

"Ah."

"It's a system."

"But not Emet?"

"I had the feeling his bar was set pretty high for, you know, messed-up personal histories."

Eden Rose picked up a pillow and held it between her chin and her collarbone while she jerked the pillowcase over it. "So he told you." With her chin low, her voice was thicker than usual.

"He told me some and I guessed some."

"And you're okay with it?" She tossed the pillow onto the bed. "That's a big bomb to drop on a first date."

"I don't know," said Mercey. She looked past Eden Rose.

Eden straightened up and brushed a strand of hair behind one ear. Mercey's shoulders were slumped, and her hands hung at her sides. "But you came to him today," said Eden Rose.

"I—didn't have anywhere else to go." Mercey bent to pick up a quilt. Her cheeks were flushed and her eyes bright. She cleared her throat as she stood up. "But yes, he told me. And you, obviously."

"I knew when I hired him," said Eden Rose.

"Is that why you hired him?"

"Whatever else he's done, he's a dream employee."

"I guess he's got a lot to prove." Mercey pulled the quilt up to the top of the bed and straightened the pillow.

"I almost wish he'd lighten up a bit on himself."

Mercey snorted.

"What?" said Eden.

"Sorry," said Mercey. "Not Emet. I was thinking—here's something I didn't tell him. Want to know why I finally put my mom in assisted living?"

"I don't know. Do I?"

"You're going to love this."

Eden Rose smiled. "Okay, I'll bite. Was it because you were working a demanding, full-time job and couldn't give her the care she needed?"

"No."

"Then why?"

"I found out Clay was stealing her meds."

"Oops."

"And you know whose fault that was?" said Mercey.

"Clay's?"

"Nope. Mine, for leaving them where he could find them."

"Really."

"My mom goes, 'You know he's sick. How could you do this to him?'"

"Wow."

"Oh, it gets better. Then, because I'd left the meds where Clay could get them, it was also my fault she didn't have enough. And when I said maybe we should lock them up, she said, 'Now, how am I supposed to manage a lock? For a college kid you're pretty stupid, Mercey. Think of *me* for a change.'"

"Ouch."

"A couple of years ago, Clay got fired from a construction job for showing up stoned," said Mercey. "He told my mom he had an accident, that he was disabled. Like, actually on disability. And she *believes* him." Mercedes flicked opened her hands as though throwing away something useless. "I'm a PT. Trust me, he's not disabled. But try telling her that."

"My guess is a lock on the meds wouldn't have helped," said Eden Rose.

"I guess."

"People do what they want to do."

Mercey bit her lip and sighed. "Emet seems different."

"Emet is different."

She sighed. "You won't tell him all this, will you?"

"No."

"I don't want to chase him away." She looked at the window. The darkness outside made the panes look solid, and the sun catcher was motionless. "Kind of a first for me."

Eden Rose sat down on the bed. "Could you tell him that?"

"No," said Mercedes, in a voice larded with *duh*.

"Why not?"

"Why should I?"

"Why shouldn't you?"

Mercey leaned down and smoothed the pillow, which did not need to be smoothed. "You don't need this—midnight info-dump."

"Nonsense," said Eden Rose. "I live for the midnight info-dump. In fact, when I got up this morning I said to my cats, 'You know what's missing in my life? A late-night confessional to curl my toes.'"

Mercey almost smiled.

"Emet told you his awful story," went on Eden Rose. "The highlights anyway. I bet you could talk to him."

"I only have lowlights." Mercey sat down on the far corner of the bed. "Okay. Look at me and look at him. Who's doing better?"

"What do you mean?"

"He's so far ahead of me."

"I'm just curious," said Eden Rose. "Do you always go shopping at the Crazy Store? It sounds like you bought out their entire stock."

Mercey stared at her lap. Her fingers grabbed each other and twisted. "Emet's been out of prison for a month," she burst out. "One month. In that time he's gotten to be friends with you and that couple in the park and even that guy who bought me that mocha this afternoon. And you're all so *nice*. I've lived here forever, and I've got my toxic family and a handful of friends whose phone numbers I don't know. Oh, God, and enough ex-boyfriends to storm the beaches at Normandy."

"So your inevitable conclusion is…?"

"He attracts nice. I attract crap."

Eden Rose nodded slowly. "Let's go into the kitchen," she said. "Do you like tea?"

Eden Rose's kitchen table was the color of old honey, except where it was punctuated by dark circles of knots. Its legs were leaf-green, round and chunky in a way that seemed matronly. A small, red bowl shaped like a strawberry contained sugar crystals the color of amber. They looked like fragments of broken glass. Eden Rose filled two mugs and set the pot down.

"These go great in tea," said Eden Rose.

"Thanks." Mercey stirred a spoonful of the brown chips into her drink.

"So what happens tomorrow?"

"Wait for a call," said Mercey. They had left voicemail and Facebook messages for her soon-to-be roommate. "When my girlfriend gets in touch we'll finish moving my stuff. Unless Clay decides to torch the house. Ha ha."

Eden sat up straight. "Do you think he would?"

"No," said Mercey. "He's an asshole, but he's never been violent."

Eden relaxed, stirring her tea. Clinking sounds drifted up from the mugs and punctuated the conversation as she and

Mercey enjoyed the privity of strangers finding themselves together in the featureless hours between midnight and dawn. Eden Rose took a sip. "Why is he doing all this to you?"

"Don't know. Don't care." She blew on her drink and took a sip. "Ooch, hot," she said, and put it down. "But he's twenty-seven and it's time to get off the teat. He's too old to be a baby and I'm too young to be his mommy." She leaned forward. "Can I tell you? I can't *wait* to have my own place."

"It's a great feeling." Eden lifted her chin in a way that took in the kitchen, the tea, the warmth on a dreary night.

"My mom's house—I feel like I'm breaking out of jail." Her hand flew to her mouth. "Oh, God. Don't tell Emet I said that."

Eden laughed. "I'm sure he's heard worse."

Mercey went back to stirring her tea. "I feel like, compared to him I don't have much to bitch about."

"Everybody's got something."

"He has more than most."

"He's an open book," said Eden Rose. "Did he tell you about his first night in prison?"

Mercedes stiffened, her hand still on the spoon.

"Two guys jumped him," said Eden Rose. "He got away, barely. But when he told me about it, you know what he said?"

"No."

"I said something vapid, like, 'How terrible,' and he said, 'Nah—they did me a favor. Up till then I thought I wanted to die.'"

Mercey let go of her spoon. The handle dinged on the rim of the mug. "See, right there. How does he do that?"

"Don't think it's been easy for him," said Eden Rose.

"But he does it," said Mercey. "I'm—some days I feel like I can't tie my own shoelaces."

"It's a journey," said Eden Rose. "Nobody's born strong."

"He is now."

"At some point most of us decide how strong we're going to be."

"I don't get Emet," said Mercey. "I don't. How can someone who looks on the bright side of—*that*—also be the guy who kills a man with one blow?"

"Beware the wrath of a patient man," said Eden Rose. "I'd hate to be around Emet if he were really angry."

"He doesn't seem angry to me."

"Or me."

Mercey went back to her tea. "I don't understand that guy. But I'm impressed."

"So am I."

"I couldn't do what he does."

"Yes, you could. Quit selling yourself short. No," Eden said when Mercey opened her mouth to protest. "My turn. Look at all you've accomplished. Look at your schooling and your career and your plans—and your dog. She's a sweetheart. There's a reason Emet likes you, you know. And don't tell him I said this, but he was scared to death to ask you out."

"I could tell."

Mercey gazed past Eden Rose and through the doorway of the kitchen. Her eyes rested again on the sun catcher in the living room window.

"I'm glad he told you about his record," said Eden Rose.

"Me, too." Mercey sighed. "Clay's not a monster, you know."

"He just plays one on TV?"

"It's the drugs."

"It's not."

"Before he started using, he was the sweetest kid," said Mercey. "One time when we were little and my mom hit me with a boot, he hid me in his room till she promised not to do it again."

"With a boot?"

"She'd just grab whatever was handy, and this time it was a big hiking boot. Metal hooks for the laces, very solid sole. She hit me on the side of the head—I literally saw stars. Well, more like the Aurora Borealis. Big sheets of light flashing." Her mouth pretended to smile, but her eyes would not. "So I…ran to Clay. And he hid me, and he made her promise."

"How old were you?"

"We were maybe nine or ten. I thought he was a superhero after that."

"Did your mom lay off you?"

"Of course not. But that's not the point."

"So he's still Clay," said Eden Rose. "The little boy is in there somewhere."

"A lost, lost little boy. Who's doing a lot of drugs."

"The drugs aren't making him do anything he doesn't want to do."

"I want him to do AA or Narcotics Anonymous. Or something."

"You can't make him go."

"Sure you can. Judges sentence people to AA all the time."

"Judges can do all kinds of things."

"But you see my point."

"Usually people have to have that rock-bottom moment." Eden Rose busied herself with her tea, pouring in a fresh cupful.

Mercey stirred her drink again. The spoon made a musical scraping sound, and she took a sip. "Can I ask you something?" she said as she put the mug down.

"Sure."

"Did you?" Mercedes indicated the sun catcher. With the window shut there was nothing to turn the little plaque, and the words "And the Wisdom to Know the Difference" glistened at them. "Did you have a rock-bottom moment?"

"I did," said Eden Rose. "It was pretty spectacular."

"So no one made you go. You had your moment, and you went."

"Hah!"

"Well, how did it happen, then? If I can ask."

Eden Rose almost laughed. "Are you kidding? Alcoholics love talking about themselves. Why do you think we get together in groups all the time?"

"To…stay sober?"

"Sucker," she said. "It's so we can blather at each other till half past never. Alcoholics are our own favorite topic. We're crazy for our pickled past. And our sobriety. How many days, years, minutes sober, and what a struggle it is."

"But—"

"We're a very chatty bunch."

Mercey smiled, and this time her eyes joined in. "So you still go to meetings."

"I do."

"What made you start?"

Eden smiled back and took a sip of tea. “My very own rock-bottom moment.”

“What…was it?”

“I woke up with a stranger and found it was me.” Her smile vanished.

“Meaning?”

Eden sighed and put down her mug. Her voice was sad and distant. “Meaning I was beyond not recognizing myself, beyond being amazed at the things I could even remember from the nights and weeks before.” Gazing past Mercey, she ran one finger around the handle of the mug as if unconscious of the small circles she was making. “I was someone else’s creature, stitched together by a drunken Dr. Frankenstein. Kidding aside. It was bad, Mercey. Really bad.”

“You must have had other bad mornings.” Mercey’s voice was neutral.

“Sure.”

“So how was this one different?”

“It landed me in the hospital.”

“Was it serious?” said Mercey.

“Even the doctors were disgusted with me.”

“How awful.”

Eden Rose stirred her tea. Mercey said nothing, and in the silence Serena yawned herself awake. She walked over to

Mercedes, putting her head in the woman's lap. Mercedes reached down to stroke the dog's glossy head. Without looking up she said, "How far along were you?"

For half the span of a heartbeat, Eden Rose's serenity splintered.

"It was early," she said. "They told me it was the size of an aspirin. An aspirin made of blood." She paused. "How did you know?"

"Hospital, waking up with a stranger that was also you. It was poetry trying to hide something."

Eden Rose rested her head on one hand. "The thing was," she said, "I couldn't remember—it wasn't just that I wasn't sure who. I didn't even know how. I had, I still have, no memory of conceiving my only child."

"Oh," said Mercey, and the soft syllable was freighted with sympathy.

"And I thought," went on Eden Rose half to herself, "the chances were so good that I'd already destroyed the little creature—alcohol poisoning and God knows what—it was a horribly easy decision."

"You don't regret it."

Eden Rose pushed the mug of tea away from herself. "I regret being in the situation in the first place," she said. "But I've never regretted the surgery."

Eden Rose made another pot of tea, Earl Greyer with extra bergamot. It was late enough that dinner was wearing off, so she put a small plate of Oreos and Chips Ahoy cookies on the table. "I started drinking after my mom died," said Eden Rose. "I was a teenager."

"Oh—that must have been terrible for you," said Mercey.

Eden nodded and took a bite of a Chips Ahoy.

"Cancer?" asked Mercey. She reached for an Oreo.

"Hit-and-run. They never caught the guy." To Mercey's horrified silence she added, "Yep. That's the usual response."

"Did you get help?"

"No. Back then kids were resilient." She took a sip of tea. "And my dad wasn't the kind to seek out assistance."

"Self-reliant?"

"Yes. He helped out by becoming an alcoholic. And me—after watching all the hell he went through with drink, watching him lose his job and his friends and seeing all the stupid, mean things it let him do—I did the same thing a couple of years later." She shook her head with a grimace. "I was so mad, I got drunk at him."

Mercedes smiled weakly. "Showed him."

"Anyway, you know the rest. I had my rock-bottom, I cleaned up, and—here we are."

Mercey looked into the amber serenity of her teacup. "Can I ask you how?"

"How what?"

"How you cleaned up." She blinked swiftly.

In the corner, Serena whimpered in her sleep. Mercey looked at her, turning away from Eden Rose.

"Is this for Clay?" said Eden Rose gently.

Mercey turned back, her eyes bird-bright. "People can change."

"If they want to."

"You didn't want to."

"I had to."

"Well, he has to, too."

Eden Rose sighed. "Mercey, I'll tell you the whole thing on one condition. You have to promise me you won't start confusing Clay and me, or thinking you can rescue him with my story. It doesn't work like that."

Mercey sat up straight. "I swear by my hope of heaven and my fear of hell."

"That's pretty good."

"Thanks. I read it somewhere. Now how did you get cleaned up?"

"Grace of God," said Eden Rose. "The intervention of a higher power."

"Can you be a little more specific?"

"Or you could call it dumb luck. Because I had no right to be that lucky. I came out of the hospital. I was a mess, I was in a lot of pain, and I was more ashamed of myself than you can imagine. I had to hold onto the wall to walk. And can you guess where I was headed?"

"To get drunk."

"Well, I'd had a hell of a day."

"So what stopped you?"

"Who," she said. "Someone stopped me. Someone I used to know but who I'd given up because he wouldn't drink with me. If he'd found me half an hour later I'd have been higher than a kite. If he'd come by a few minutes earlier I'd have still been in the hospital. But there he was, and he stopped me and asked me if I was all right. And maybe because no one had asked me that in a very long time, I told him everything."

"And?"

"And he said, 'Come with me.' And we went to his AA meeting." She laughed. "I thought they were the most pathetic bunch of whiners I'd ever met, but it was raining and there were free cookies, so I stayed. At the end of the meeting he introduced me to his friend Joshua and asked him to hire me at his coffeehouse. And Josh said, 'Ninety days, ninety meetings, no second chances. You come in late, you're fired. You don't show, you're fired. Come in clean and presentable. Don't even think about coming in drunk. And get a sponsor.' And he walked away."

Mercey tilted her head. "I don't get it."

"He meant he would hire me provisionally for ninety days if I attended an AA meeting every one of those days."

"Wow."

"Yes."

"And you did it."

"I did. With damned poor grace, at first."

"So, wait—was the coffeehouse Serve You Right?"

"It was."

"This sounds like the employment equivalent of a shotgun wedding."

"What else was I going to do?" said Eden Rose. "My dad was out of the picture by then. I was about to be evicted from my apartment, and now I had medical expenses too. So I figured I would play their little game and make a little money, and then I could go back to drinking in peace and quiet."

"But you didn't."

"No, because my sponsor was a real bitch. She told me never to call her when I was drunk and never to miss a meeting. I hated all of it. I hated the meetings and I hated the people. They talked in bumper stickers— 'One Day at a Time' and all that." She laughed again. "I was so superior, practically homeless and fresh off an abortion. And they saw right through me, damn them."

"And that's how you started working at the coffee shop."

"Yes." Eden Rose put her teacup down. "It helped me almost as much as the meetings."

"Because you had a job?"

"Partly," she said. "But I think moderation was part of it too. I'd lost track of that."

"Of moderation?"

"Look," said Eden Rose, "you have to understand one thing. As a career drunkard, I never want a drink, ever."

"You don't?"

"I want ten."

"I don't understand that."

"No one does."

"Okay," said Mercey. "Go on."

"So working at the café, it occurred to me one day that I was setting a table, not a trough."

"A trough."

"I didn't need to supply unlimited food, coffee, napkins, whatever. I could give someone *enough.* And suddenly I saw that most of the time, enough was enough. It didn't need to be more than enough. And as that realization hit me, another one rolled in. I saw there was something about feeding people that fed my soul. I'd been such a parasite…and now I—wasn't."

Mercey put her mug down and reached for another Oreo. "It sounds like the place really spoke to you."

"Literally."

Mercedes blinked. "Excuse me?"

"One day I was in the storeroom at Serve You Right," said Eden Rose. "This was before it was my place. I was just coming around to the idea that maybe all these mean, rotten people who were interfering with my drinking schedule might be on to something. And also that the fact that my life was such a mess might have a little bit to do with the choices I'd been making. Anyway, Josh sent me out back to get some spices, and I didn't know where they were so I was moving stuff around trying to find them. And I saw a jar of relish, and the light was hitting it just so, and it was the most vibrant green you can imagine. Just like a forest in springtime, all tiny leaves bursting with big promises. And the label suddenly looked like an imperative. *Relish!*"

Mercey lifted her cup so it hid her smile. “I see.”

Eden Rose grinned at her. “Wait for it. Because right next to it, but turned a little so I couldn’t see the whole label, was a jar of savory. So the two together said, *‘Relish! Savor!’* And I thought, dear God in Heaven, the very condiments are telling me to embrace life. How could I say no?” She threw back her head and laughed.

“Colonel Mustard,” gasped Mercey, “in the storeroom with an aphorism.” And she dissolved in a cascade of giggles.

Sunday, September 21

Hours of Operation:

8:00 am to 5:00 pm

22

Sunday, September 21: The Fall Equinox.

Today, at 10:52 am, autumn officially begins.

As one season tips into another and everything changes, we celebrate with today's special, the first homemade apple pie of the year.

(Secret ingredient: mists and mellow fruitfulness.)

As Eden Rose stepped off the chair, the door opened and Emet walked in. "Morning," he said.

"Barely." Eden Rose wiped down the chair and returned it to its table. She yawned.

Emet looked at her. "Tired? You?"

"Mercey and I were up late last night," she said, and yawned again. "What's the coffee of the day again? Never mind—I'll just chew on the beans."

"How's she doing?"

"Better. Her girlfriend saw the Facebook message and called at my place. They're going to drive to Mercey's house to finish the move this morning instead of tonight. Serena's staying at my apartment till then."

Emet pulled on his apron. "Did she say anything about me?"

"Yeah, she told me to pass you a note in gym class."

"Just asking."

"So ask her, doofus."

"Okay, boss lady." He glanced at the blackboard. "Wow. I guess I'm making pie right about now." He tucked his hair into his hairnet, stepped behind the counter, and pulled out canisters of flour and sugar.

"The butter's already softened," said Eden Rose. "I got three kinds of apples. The Macouns and Honeycrisps are organic; the Spencers are conventional. If there's enough, can you keep them separate?"

"So, some organic pie and some regular?"

"Yes."

"No problem."

Emet set to work. Under his swift fingers, peel fell away from apples in rippling bands, like banners unfurling. The flesh of the fruit was moonglow streaked with green. His knife flashed through handfuls of rosemary, reducing the needles to pillows of emerald fluff. He scraped two lemons clean, and their zest drifted to the counter in curling threads of sunlight. Clouds of spice filled the air, cinnamon and nutmeg and clove, their perfume brown and aromatic.

Emet topped the Spencer pie with a lattice crust and set it on the counter next to the oven. For the organic pies, he rolled a velvet-soft circle of dough and punched out leaves with cookie cutters the size of half-dollars: oak, maple, beech. He scattered them atop the apple filling and glazed them with beaten egg yolk, so that when they emerged from the oven in an hour and a half they would glow gold and brown amid the bubbling juices.

Meanwhile, Eden Rose emptied and washed the vases on the walls. She filled them with water and loaded each with an exuberance of mums: pom-pom, anemone, quill, spider, thistle, and double-blooms, all in shades of butter and saffron that glowed against the dark, brick walls. She arranged the day's pastries in the glass display case and set three kinds of coffee percolating. Finally, she flipped the Closed sign and opened the door. The customers walked in, stopped, and breathed deeply of the sweet, autumnal vapor that hung in the air promising new things; and as they walked forward to line up at the counter they smiled at Emet and Eden Rose because they knew they were where they should be.

Emet and Eden served coffee and pie and breakfast as the sun rose in the sky and the clock hands stretched toward mid-morning. The line was short and moved briskly.

"Coffee, please," said a familiar voice. "And can you leave room for cream and sugar?"

Emet's face flashed with happiness. His hands leaped to assemble the order as Eden Rose busied herself at the far end of the counter. "Thought you didn't drink coffee."

"I don't," said Mercey. Her eyes were tired but cheerful, and she wore her clothes from the day before. "It's for my girlfriend. She's circling the block."

"City won't let us put in a drive-through," said Emet. "Flavor?"

"Good. Gives me an excuse to come in." Mercey squinted at the board. "Jeeze. Um…Kenyan Gold?"

Emet filled the cup three-quarters full and slipped a java jacket onto it, handing it to her along with the lid. She paid. Their fingers brushed, and they spoke in delighted unison.

"Can I see you tonight?"

Mercey laughed. Emet grinned, incandescent. "After work," he said at exactly the same time Mercey said, "After I move."

"Ahem," said a woman with a severe grey haircut who was next in line.

"Cream and sugar?" said Mercey.

"Behind you," said Emet. "Pizza?"

"Where?"

"Ahem."

"Tonight. I can still bring pizza."

"It's a date."

"It is?"

"Evidently," said the grey-haired woman. "Coffee, black." Emet filled a cup and handed it to her. She gave him exact change and left, her heels snapping on the floor.

Mercey glanced out the door. "Gotta go. See you tonight," she called over her shoulder. "Oh, hi, Gene."

"Good morning." Gene held the door for Mercey before striding in, full of purpose. "And good morning to you too."

"Nice to see you again," said Eden Rose. "What can I get you?"

"A cup of coffee and an artery-clogging snack should clear my debt," he said. "What do you suggest?"

"We have a couple pieces of pie left," said Emet. He was still smiling and had a vaguely anesthetized look as he pointed to the case. "This one's organic."

"Oh, no, I don't eat that organic stuff," said the man. "I figure the more preservatives I get in me, the longer I'll take to die."

"One hunk of pesticides, coming up," said Emet, opening the case.

"Builds character," said Gene. "What coffee do you recommend?"

"Columbian," said Eden Rose. "The acidity is a counterpoint to the sweetness of the pie."

Gene took his cup of coffee and sat at an empty table, nodding to a red-eyed college student who was peering, vulture-like, at the screen of her laptop and clacking on the keyboard like Ann Miller proving herself to a skeptical director. Emet came to the table with the pie. Apples cascaded from under the lattice crust in a fragrant avalanche that gleamed with brown sugar sauce. Tendrils of nutmeg-scented mist drifted from the surface. "Warmed it up for you," he said.

"Thank you, young man. I appreciate good service." Gene took a forkful of apples, blew on it, and put it in his mouth. He moaned and shut his eyes momentarily, then swallowed.

"Marry me," he begged. "My wife will understand."

Emet laughed. "I'm flattered. But I don't think my girlfriend is quite so liberal-minded."

Clay drove fast. “Hit hard and run,” he chanted. “Say who I am. Tell him he can’t fuck with me like this.” He practiced. “Shut up. Fuck you. Leave me alone.”

He had spent the night at Adam’s house. He had drunk Adam’s beer and smoked Adam’s joints and eaten Adam’s food. And he had borrowed Adam’s car, reasoning that Adam understood, or would once he noticed his car was missing. They had a brief conversation about it. Adam said, “Dude. You are too fucked up to drive.” Then he left the room, and Clay said, “Wrong. I’m fucked up enough to do whatever I want,” and took Adam’s keys from the roach clip that was bent into a hook and nailed to the doorjamb.

A clatter of empty bottles on the car floor jangled every time he turned a corner or changed speed. For Clay, alcohol was rectitude and audacity and all the luck of a carjacker with an AK-47. It was unfiltered philter, and with it he could not fail.

“Everyone thinks they deserve more than me,” he said aloud. “Fuck them. I’ll show them.”

Clay gripped the steering wheel and held onto angry fistfuls of breath as he drove toward Railroad Street.

Mercey's girlfriend dropped her off and left with the first load of boxes. Alone in her bedroom, Mercey was taping shut the last carton when it occurred to her that Clay might have left her phone in his room. She put down the roll of tape and walked downstairs.

"Clay?" She stood at the top of the basement stairs and flipped on the light. No one answered, and after a moment she descended the stairs, stepping into the dark entity of the house and its subterranean forces.

All that was unwashed about Clay had settled here: mottled socks, threadbare tee shirts, and Coke cans half-full of flat soda and cigarette butts. Mercey wrinkled her nose. Gingerly she lifted the cushions from the decaying sofa, then put them back. She shuffled through the candy wrappers and take-out boxes on the coffee table, and, trying to come into as little contact with the carpet as possible, knelt down and peered under the table and sofa. The phone was nowhere in evidence, so she walked over to his desk and looked in the drawers and behind stacks of CDs and DVD-ROMs. The computer was still on.

"Did you sell it on Ebay?" muttered Mercey. "Trade it to one of your junkie buddies?" She rolled the mouse. The screen lit up.

> *Ok men here is the plan I am going to take care of that jailbird. Need him out of the picture. It will hapn no mistake*

Mercey sat on the stained desk chair and scrolled down. Her eyes widened.

> *...at his place?*
>
> *...tried that...*
>
> *...where he works is better dude. He wrk Sunday?*
>
> *...yah good point I will go there!!!*
>
> *...hey Claymation you know what would be cool is if u filmed it we can post it after!!!!!!!!!! Lol!!!!!!!!*
>
> *...haha it will be a sight worth seeing I promise u. Gonna be D Day at the cafe! I will be a free man soon. LMAO!!!!*

"You *bastard.*" Flame-hot anger lit Mercey's cheeks. She leaped to her feet, a phoenix of rage. Mercedes dashed up the stairs and flew out the door.

Clay rammed the car over the curb, denting the right front rim. The bumper screamed over the concrete. He spilled his bulk onto the sidewalk and hurled open the door to the coffee shop.

At the counter, Eden Rose was changing a coffee filter. Clay stood over her, blocking the light. He wore a baggy, black tee shirt with the name of a video arcade on it, and around his neck was a plastic, glow-in-the-dark crucifix. His brows were knurled with rage.

Eden Rose slid the coffee filter into place and snapped the compartment shut. "Good to see you again," she said.

"Shut up," he said. There were only four customers, and Clay's voice clanged in the almost-empty room. A middle-aged couple in hiking boots and matching green windbreakers started.

Gene put down his fork. "Is there a problem here?" he said.

"You're goddamn right there's a problem," shouted Clay. "Where's that lowlife who's been fucking my sister?"

"What are you talking about?" said Eden Rose.

"You heard me," said Clay. His shoulders were hunched and tight.

Emet emerged from the back room, carrying a tray of freshly iced scones. "Emet," said Eden Rose severely, "are you aware of any lowlife fucking this man's sister?"

“Couldn’t be me,” he said, putting down the tray. “I never even held her hand.”

“So you two know each other,” said Eden Rose.

“Not exactly,” said Emet. “But I’m guessing he’s Mercey’s brother Clay. He lives in her basement.”

Gene snorted. Clay lurched around, glaring.

“Shut up,” said Clay to Gene. “Fuck you.”

Gene put down his fork. Clay was between him and the exit, and he did not move. The couple in matching windbreakers slipped out. The door banged behind them. Clay jumped at the sound. He took a step toward Gene, who appeared to be studying him intently. Gene’s hand closed over his fork.

“I’m also thinking he might be the guy who came by my place yesterday morning,” said Emet loudly. Clay whipped back at the sound of his voice.

“Really?” said Eden Rose. “Why?”

“He knows my name, and he doesn’t seem to like me very much.”

“Good point,” said Eden Rose. “Bart would know.”

“I wonder if he’s home,” said Emet.

The young woman with the laptop closed her computer and silently lifted her cell phone, framing Clay in the screen. She tapped it, and the phone began to film.

“We’ve had dealings, too,” said Eden Rose.

"You and Clay?" said Emet.

"Yes."

"Leave me alone," said Clay. He directed his glower at Emet. "And stay the fuck away from my sister." He pounded the counter. A piece of coffee cake trembled off its platter.

"Yeah?" said Emet. "I think she gets to decide that." His voice was neutral, it was a statement of fact; but his body was tensed.

Gene sat at his table, so still he was almost the color of air. Eden Rose looked at him, and shifted her eyes toward the door and back again. Gene barely shook his head. He frowned.

"Get out here," said Clay. He grabbed some wrapped cookies and threw them to the floor. "Quit hiding, you chickenshit."

"Hey," said Eden Rose.

"No need to throw stuff," said Emet.

"I'll throw more than *stuff* if you don't get out here, you sick bastard." Clay's flabby arm swept a cake stand onto the floor. A pyramid of molasses snickerdoodles scattered sparkles of sugar onto the brown boards, and the thick, glass cover rolled in a tight circle behind Clay's feet with a sound like bells. "Be a man. Be a *man."*

Emet's eyes had gone terribly dark. He pulled off his apron with a single, flowing movement and slid around the counter.

He stopped outside of Clay's reach, his fury contained; but something within him swept to and fro like a fire, full of changing lights.

Clay stepped forward. He raised a fist. "I am going to hit you so bad you go away forever." He was breathing hard, triumphant. "If you hit me back, I'll tell the cops and you'll go back and rot in jail where you belong, you sack of shit."

"I don't think so," said Emet. His voice was light, but he kept his weight on the balls of his feet, and his hands, though empty, were ready. He held himself like a man who had seen danger before.

"You think I won't hit you?" Clay shook his fist again.

"I think you'll try," said Emet. "But if you hit me, I will hit back."

"Shut up."

"I'll also press charges for assault."

"Shut *up.*"

"I have witnesses. You will lose."

"Fuck you."

"You think prison was bad for me? It was."

"Shut up. Fuck you."

"But it would be worse for you."

"Shut up. Fuck you. Leave me alone." Clay was almost chanting.

"Guys like you do not do very well behind the wall, my friend."

"Who do you think the cops will believe—me, or some ex-con who already killed one guy over a girl?"

Gene shot a quick look at Emet.

"Let's find out," said Eden Rose.

Clay gave a start. "Huh?"

"Call the cops," she said. "Right now. I believe you have your sister's cell phone." As Clay continued to stare at her she added, "Unless, of course, you prefer to pay for the rubber check you wrote me last week, and all the fees associated with it." She pointed to the voided check taped to the cash register.

"I never been in here before," said Clay. He did not look at the check.

"You were wearing a baseball cap last time, and a different shirt," said Eden Rose. "Maybe you thought I wouldn't recognize you."

Gene studied Clay. "Recognize you," he echoed. He slowly stood.

Clay turned at the sound of his voice. "Who the fuck are you?" The college student shifted her phone to put Gene in the frame as he walked toward the bigger, younger man.

"Gene," said Emet under his breath. *"Gene."*

"I'm the sucker whose wallet you stole," said Gene. Like Emet, he stopped just beyond Clay's reach. Gene's mouth was tight and angry. "I remember you. You were behind me in line at the gas station."

Emet. Gene. Eden Rose. Clay stood in the middle of a triangle of people who saw him as he was: brutal, yes, but also ridiculous and somehow impotent, like a golem made of custard. He slapped his hands over his ears. "Shut up," he cried. "Fuck you. Leave me alone." He turned in a slow circle, trying to get away from their eyes and their horrible knowledge. His face was made of nightmares. He staggered to the wall and fell back against it, his head rocking from side to side. His ear bumped one of the vases, and water slapped onto his shoulder.

The door flew open and Mercedes burst in, gasping. "Clay," she cried. "Don't."

The emptiness in Clay's eyes grew hard, became absence visible. "Bitch."

"Don't hurt them."

"Him? Don't hurt *him!*"

Mercey stepped forward, trying to even out her breathing. "Clay. It's okay."

Clay gave a broken whinny of a laugh. "Sure it is."

"I mean it."

"Nothing's okay as long as you and that shit are ruining my life."

"I'm not mad at you," said Mercey.

"Liar. Liar. Liar." Clay's hands opened and closed. Mercey took another step forward.

"I can get help for you," she said.

"I don't need any *help*, bitch."

"Okay. You don't need any help," she said. "Let's go home and talk, okay?"

Clay blinked. "Go home?"

"Yes. We'll just leave."

"Just leave," he repeated.

"Yes. It's okay, Clay. I love you."

Clay shoved himself away from the wall. "Fuck you, bitch," he roared. "You are *always leaving me!"*

He yanked the vase from its sconce and hurled it. Mercey whipped to one side. It hit the wall next to her. Glass exploded in a fountain of starlight and broken flowers, falling away into darkness. *"Shit!"* she cried.

Clay staggered toward her.

Emet moved like a panther made of shadows. He seized a stainless steel milk canister with both hands. Turning, he smashed it down on Clay's head with one smooth motion.

Clay's knees buckled. They hit the floor. He gaped at Emet in bewilderment. His eyes rolled back in his head, and his torso crashed to the ground.

Emet stood over him, holding the canister.

Mercedes stared from Emet to her brother and made a little sound, as though she were swallowing something.

Outside, a breeze seethed in the leaves with a sound like applause.

The door swung open, and Marty the cop and his partner walked in.

Seeing them, Emet set the canister on the floor and slowly raised his hands above his head.

The time on the college student's videophone was exactly 10:52.

Epilogue

"Now, this is perfect, young First," said Isadore. "Just the right blend of sweet and tart."

"Thanks," said Emet. The four of them sat on their accustomed park benches, surrounded by the moth-flecked darkness of the fading day. Eden Rose jotted in her notebook, flipping to a new page.

Daisy wiped her fingers on a paper napkin. "And what a lovely way to celebrate your return," she said to Emet. "It's so good to have you back."

"Same here," said Emet.

"How are you holding up, son?" said Isadore.

"I'm okay," said Emet. "Two weeks I can handle."

"I couldn't believe it when they arrested you," said Eden Rose. "I thought they should have pinned a medal on you."

"Guess they were all out of medals," said Emet.

"How did you get out?" asked Isadore.

Emet grinned. "I stole a spoon," he intoned, "and every night between midnight and dawn I dug a secret tunnel to the sewer system."

"How very resourceful of you," marveled Daisy.

"Stunk like a dozen pigs," he said solemnly.

"Where did you hide the spoon?" she said.

"You don't want to know." Emet's eyes widened to indicate unutterable suffering.

"Oh, *my.*" Daisy lifted her hand to her mouth. Isadore gave a craggy smile.

"Moving right along," said Eden Rose. She reached into the bag and pulled out a croissant. "This one is more savory," she said. "Mushroom and a blend of cheeses."

"Ooh! Me, me, me!" cried Daisy. Eden Rose handed it to her and she bit into the flaky pastry with her eyes alight.

"You didn't waste any time getting back to work," said Isadore.

"I got in last night," said Emet. "Saw Mercey this morning before she went in to the clinic."

"Did you bring her flowers, dear?"

"Biggest bouquet I could get at Stop and Shop."

Isadore nodded approvingly. "Well done, Emet First."

"I figured it was hard to go wrong that way," said Emet.

"She's missed you," said Daisy.

"We all have," said Eden Rose. "Customers too."

"Thanks," said Emet. "Good to be back."

"How did you manage to get out really?" said Daisy.

"They did an investigation and I had a hearing," said Emet.

“They decided there were extenuating circumstances,” said Eden Rose.

“I thought I was sc—” Emet cleared his throat. “In there for good.”

“Your young lady said she spoke with your parole officer,” said Isadore.

“Yeah, she did,” said Emet. “But I think they filed her under crazy girlfriend, you know? It was like, ‘We’ll bear that in mind, kind of.’”

“Turns out that KO’ing even the most degenerate citizens is a parole violation,” said Eden Rose. “Who knew?”

“My PO was definitely aware of that,” said Emet.

“Marty talked to them,” said Eden Rose.

“That helped,” said Emet. “A lot, I think.”

“We were all backing you up,” said Eden. “Clay had it coming. It might have been okay without Marty.”

“Maybe,” said Emet. “Maybe not.”

“Well, you’re back home where you belong, dear, and that’s what matters,” said Daisy.

“And I picked a good night for it,” said Emet. The evening was clear, on the tipping point between warm and cool, but still pleasant enough that the park was comfortable. From the playground came the sound of a mother’s voice cajoling a child before they both dissolved into laughter, the boy's peals high and delighted, rising above his mother's chuckles.

"Are you going to the town meeting, Emet First?" inquired Isadore. Eden Rose had shut down the café early so she could go.

"Got other plans," said Emet.

"Isadore's going to disrupt it," said Daisy through her mouthful. Her voice bubbled with pride.

"Why?" said Emet.

"Because the cabal of bloated attorneys that run this burg need to be reminded that not everyone is in lock-step with them." Isadore drew himself up straight and thrust his chin out like a Roman orator.

"Uh?"

"This year we're protesting the excise tax on bicycles," said Daisy. "It's so exciting."

"On education, you mean," roared Isadore.

"I'll just repeat myself," said Emet. "Uh?"

"Worthington College owns 42% of the land in Oxbridge, and being a non-profit they don't pay taxes on it," said Eden Rose. "The first- and second-year students aren't allowed to have cars on campus, so everyone has a bike. The town legislature is trying to pass an excise tax on bicycles to make up for what they see is a shortfall—"

"Do you know how many jobs that college provides?" thundered Isadore. "Not to mention this is penalizing young people who are trying to get a decent education."

"Ruthie's bringing a bunch of her friends," said Eden Rose. "I imagine you'll see them at the meeting. She's organizing a bicycle brigade to impede traffic."

"Collectively speaking," said Isadore, "the town legislature is one big Lady Astor's horse."

Daisy giggled into her croissant, then set it down on the napkin on her lap. "We go every year," she said. "Isadore shouts and waves the Constitution around, and the council members tell him to leave. When he won't, Marty wrestles him to the ground and pulls him bodily out the door. I film it. Then we go over to our daughter's and she throws the whole thing up on YouTube." She beamed at Emet. "I just adore social media, don't you?"

"You let yourself get beat up by a cop every year?" said Emet.

"Certainly not," said Isadore.

"Marty is our man on the inside, dear."

"After we leave Town Hall, we go bowling," said Isadore.

"Isadore usually wins," said Daisy.

"Wiped the alley with him last three years running," said Isadore smugly.

"How about you?" said Emet to Daisy. "Do you ever shout and stand on chairs?"

"No, dear. I tried it once or twice, but…" she sighed deeply.

"Marty," groaned Isadore.

"What?" said Emet.

"He's too much of a gentleman to thrash me about," said Daisy. "He just gave me his arm and walked me out the door."

"The whole thing looked more like a cotillion than an exercise in civil disobedience," grumped Isadore.

Emet ran his fingers lightly over the knuckles of one hand. "Do you even have a bike?" he asked.

"It's the principle!" bellowed Isadore. "Some things are worth fighting for, young man."

"I think Emet knows that, dearest," said Daisy.

"Of course," said Isadore. "No offense meant, young man."

"Oh, hey. None taken."

"And how are the young lady and her degenerate brother?" said Isadore.

"She's okay," said Emet. "He's in pretty deep."

"His attorney talked him out of a trial," said Eden Rose. "Between all the witnesses and the stuff online, he'd left a pretty detailed schematic of his intentions."

"Which makes it conspiracy, I'll be bound," said Isadore.

"And Bart ID'd him right away too," said Eden Rose. "Is there such a thing as attempted breaking and entering?"

"The checkbook thing is larceny right there," said Emet.

"The worst part for me is the animal cruelty," said Daisy. "Disgusting man."

"That should be a felony, if you ask me," said Isadore.

"I think it is," said Eden Rose. "If they want it to be."

"And he threw a vase at his sister," said Daisy. "Talk about sibling rivalry."

"Or aggravated assault," said Emet. "With witnesses, on video."

"That's my favorite bit," Isadore chuckled. "Young reprobate blasts into the coffee shop like Mephistopheles with a bee in his pants, and ends up immortalized onscreen."

"Such quick thinking on her part," said Daisy admiringly.

"She figured she couldn't get past him to the door, and she couldn't call 911 without his hearing it," said Eden Rose. "She showed me the video—it's good quality."

"I expect he's not at all videogenic," said Daisy.

"What he lacks in charisma, he makes up in drama," said Eden Rose. "The video is hot stuff."

"Saved my behind," said Emet.

"How so, dear?" said Daisy.

"Well, first off, the DA saw it," said Emet.

"He laughed till he wet his lapels," interjected Eden Rose.

"Right," said Emet. "Which is why he, um, declined to bring charges. Against me, I mean. And then he talked to the parole board. So between that and Marty and everything else—"

"Here you are, safe and sound," said Daisy brightly. "I do like happy endings." Her green eyes sparkled like dew on summer grass.

"I hope she kept the video," said Isadore. "Show the grandkids how to stand up to a bull in a china shop."

"She emailed it to herself," said Emet.

"To have a copy, dear?" said Daisy.

"She knew the cops would confiscate the phone."

"Outrageous," muttered Isadore. "Penalizing an active citizen."

"I expect they need it for evidence, dear," said Daisy, laying a soothing hand on Isadore's sleeve.

"Poppycock. They could have used a reprint, couldn't they? She ought to get herself a good attorney and see what the law actually says."

"Perhaps at the moment she's more interested in getting herself a replacement phone," said Daisy. "Priorities, love."

"Done and done," said Emet.

"We took up a collection for her," said Eden Rose. "Word got out fast. There was enough for a smart phone by closing Monday."

"Want to know the irony?" said Emet. "She's a criminal justice major."

"No!" said Daisy in delight.

"Junior year at Worthington," said Emet. "And that paper she was working on? Video technologies for law enforcement."

"Goodness to gracious."

"I think she has enough material for her thesis now," said Eden Rose.

"Didn't he also steal a car?" said Daisy.

"His friend doesn't want to press charges," said Emet.

"Bart's thrilled with the whole thing," said Eden Rose. "He's writing an epic poem about it. The working title is, 'The Crapulous Sanctimony of the November Man.'"

"The whaty what of the who?" said Emet.

"Meaning Clay was drunk and full of it," said Eden Rose. "Bart sees him as a toxic anti-hero hoisted on his own petard. The first lines are, 'None are so hopelessly enslaved/As those who falsely believe they are free.'"

"That's really good," said Emet.

"Yes, Goethe thought so too when he wrote it."

"Oops."

"So Bart's using it as an epigram instead," said Eden Rose.

"How clever," said Daisy. "It's too good to throw away."

"I've known Bart since he had a last name," said Isadore. "He's no plagiarist."

"He'd read it somewhere and forgotten. Honest mistake," said Eden Rose.

"Bart's from around here?" said Emet. "I thought he was British."

"Good Lord, no," said Isadore. "Born in Pittsfield, raised in Great Barrington. He went to an Ivy college on the GI Bill and came back with that accent and a degree in classics."

"He taught at the Newcastle School for years," said Eden Rose. "But he's one of us. Bart just talks a good BBC."

"Live and learn," said Emet.

"People aren't always as they seem," said Daisy.

"Just usually," said Emet.

"Well, your young lady seems darling," said Daisy.

"I'm seeing her tonight," said Emet. "She's going to show me her new place."

"How lovely," said Daisy. "When all's said and done, I just knew she would like you if you gave her a chance." To Emet's silence she added, "And how are *you* in all this, dear one?"

Emet gave a laugh that sounded like black sandpaper. "Are you kidding me?"

“Not especially, dear.”

“I just got out of jail for the second time in six weeks. I’m an ex-con with a high school diploma, and I’m dating a doctor. I’m scared shi—”

Isadore pulled himself straight as an oak. “There are ladies present,” he barked.

“—shirtless,” concluded Emet. “What did you think I was going to say, Isadore?”

Isadore shook a finger at Emet as Daisy’s giggles garlanded the night.

“Degrees aren’t everything,” said Eden Rose.

“Yeah,” said Emet, “but she has so *many.*”

“Perhaps,” said Daisy, wiping her eyes with her napkin, “you had best let the young lady decide for herself about you. It could be that you have things to offer that a diploma doesn’t.”

“She’s a sweetheart,” said Eden Rose.

“Her family is a nightmare,” said Emet. “Honest to God.”

“They do take the fun right out of dysfunctional,” admitted Eden Rose.

“I don’t get how she came out so nice,” said Emet.

“Some plants grow best in poor soil, dear,” said Daisy.

“Meaning what?” said Emet. “She likes me because I’m more poor soil?”

“Don’t be a noodnik, dear.”

"Sorry," said Emet. "Didn't mean to get defensive."

"Of course not," said Daisy. "No, her roots are where they are, and that can't be your worry. But she seems to be growing toward a new light these days."

"Mm."

"I imagine her situation with you could feel rather new and strange."

"Why?" said Emet. "I was thinking about this while I was—I mean, if you've met the right person—or *a* right person—can't you tell?"

"Oh, no, dear. Not necessarily."

"It's supposed to feel right. What does it mean if it feels weird?"

Isadore chuckled. "'Supposed to,'" he said. "Now, there are two words that will lead you down the primrose path."

"What he means, dear," said Daisy, "is for heaven's sake, forget what things are supposed to be like and see if they're right for you." She leaned against her husband of almost half a century. His arm went around her. "When Isadore and I started dating, the whole thing felt curiouser and curiouser. At least for me."

"Yeah?"

"I was used to tempestuous young men who seemed romantic because of their secrets. Whereas my current gentleman caller here is quite different from that." She smiled at Isadore, who smiled back. "So I said to myself, 'Daisy Greene, this feels new and different because it *is* new and different. Just see where it takes you.' And I did."

"This girl of yours," said Isadore. "Do you love her?"

Emet blushed. "Ah...."

"One day at a time," said Eden Rose.

"Like," said Daisy. "Do you like her, Emet?"

"Definitely," said Emet. "Even though it's curiouser and curiouser."

"Well, there you go, dear," said Daisy. "And I wouldn't fret about her family too much. A rose that grows in a compost heap is still a rose."

Eden checked her watch. "Town meeting starts in twenty minutes," she said. She crumpled her empty bag into a ball and reached for the spotted and wrinkled napkins before tossing them into the trashcan. Isadore stood and gave his hand to Daisy, who took it as she rose to her feet.

"Will we see you tomorrow, dear?" she said.

"Sure," said Emet. "Have a good night."

"We always do, love." She smiled at Isadore as they walked away. Her voice drifted over the dabble and splash of the fountain. "Remember that time you forced a recount? I was *so* proud."

Emet stretched his legs out and leaned back against the bench. Above the bright haze of the park lights, the sky was an inverted cup of liquid indigo in whose depths a single star gleamed like a droplet of light.

Mercey walked out of the shadows and sat down next to him, letting her purse slip off her shoulder. "Hey."

"Hey." He smiled. "How was work?"

"Good. You?"

"Same. We closed early for the town meeting."

"Oh, right. I should go to one of those."

"From what Daisy tells me, it's great entertainment value."

"Some other year," said Mercey. They rested for a moment, and the silence between them was as soft as the light of the dusk.

"How's Clay?" said Emet presently. Mercey's brother was staying rent-free at the county jail in Oxbridge while his lawyer and the District Attorney haggled over his fate.

"I saw him today. He's still mad at you for getting him arrested, but the withdrawal symptoms are my fault. So pretty average, I'd say."

Emet glanced at her. "He gonna stay mad?"

"Probably. But it doesn't matter if he's—in there." She looked away. "Worry about it when he gets out. I guess."

Emet shifted on the bench. "You know I can't be around him."

"He's my *brother*, Emet." Mercey's tone sharpened. It was half bellicosity, half a plea for him to hold her and tell her he understood.

"No, I mean—it's part of my parole."

"What is?"

"No consorting with known criminals."

Mercey flinched. "It's just Clay."

"They can throw me back in. For good."

She sighed and stared away. "I didn't realize." And the silence that had been so easy grew brittle.

Emet spoke first. "I'm sorry."

"For what?"

"All of it."

"You didn't make the rules."

"True," he said, and they both relaxed.

"I know who Clay is," she said. "Trust me, I have no illusions. This was a long time coming."

"Tends to catch up with people."

"Sure did this time."

"He was on a tear."

"He's still getting headaches," said Mercey. "The doctor says it might be a few weeks."

Emet winced. "That one really is my fault."

"Not by my count," she said. "He swung first."

"True." Emet paused. "You should visit him, though."

"I just did."

"No, I mean—he's looking at a lot of years."

She flinched.

"Visits. You don't know what it means," went on Emet.

"Why?"

Emet sighed. "You're inside. There's a wall. And you know everyone else is on the other side of it, going to the movies and writing Christmas cards and deciding what they want to wear that day. For a couple of months people write and visit. Then after a while they don't. And part of you says, okay, it's not easy coming here, it's a scary place, they search all the visitors, some people really hate that. And part of you says, the hell with a visit, no one has five minutes to write me a postcard? 'Cause mostly no one does. After a while. And you feel—like you're buried somewhere, still breathing."

Mercedes stared at him. "Oh, God," she said, and dropped her face into her hands.

"Sorry," said Emet again.

She drew a shuddering breath and put her hands down. Her face was tight. "No, don't be. I'd rather know the truth. Clay won't admit he's in trouble. He still thinks he can walk away from this."

"Why?"

"He always has."

"Not this time," said Emet.

"No."

They sighed together and half-laughed at their unison. The darkness thrummed with cricketsong and the liquid percussion of the fountain.

Mercey cleared her throat. "One thing I was wondering."

"What?"

"Why wouldn't you let me see you? If visits are so important."

Following his arrest, Emet had been transported to a maximum-security prison at the other end of the state, in a process the inmates called "taking trips." He and half a dozen freshly convicted felons were loaded into a windowless van with a long plastic bench running along each side. A dirty skylight, locked shut and shielded with a grate, gave the only light. Manacles bit painfully into Emet's ankles, and his hands were cuffed to a chain around his waist. He and the other men were shackled to each other, and each time the van went around a corner or into a pothole they all braced their feet on the floor so as not to drag the entire group off the bench. The van smelled of vomit, urine, and disinfectant. One of the men was crying and trying not to.

Emet stared fixedly at the fountain. His eyes were lightless, and shadows painted his cheekbones. "Long drive for you," he said.

Mercey waited. "And?" she said presently.

"And," he said, "I never wanted you to see me in a grey shirt with DOC stamped on the back."

Mercey looked down and plucked at a loose thread on her shirt. "I wouldn't have cared."

"I would."

She straightened up and tossed her hair over her shoulders. "What if they had revoked your parole?"

"That didn't happen."

"But if it had?"

"It didn't."

Mercey's lips barely curved. "Got me there, Einstein."

Emet gave a dim smile. His fingers drifted over his knuckles. "Hey, my turn. Can I ask you something?"

"Sure."

"This probably isn't the best time."

"And yet here we are. Ask already."

He cleared this throat. "What in the world do you see in me?"

"Other than the fact that you're the dead opposite of my brother?" She kept her tone light.

Emet did not. "Most guys aren't your brother," he said. "You could have a doctor or a lawyer or anything you wanted. What do you see in a guy like me?"

She almost laughed. "Emet. Are you serious?"

"Yes."

She tucked her hair behind one ear. "Okay, then. Why do you cook?"

"What does that—"

"Work with me," she said. "What do you like about cooking?"

"You're pushy, Dr. Finch."

"Don't I know it."

Emet leaned back against the bench and considered. "I like making something from nothing," he said finally. "You take a bunch of stuff no one could eat, and you put it together right, and you get food. And it works again the next time. As long as you know your oven and you have your ingredients and your tools, it'll always come out."

"Reliable magic."

"Kind of."

Mercey leaned her cheek on one hand, her elbow resting on the back of the park bench. "I can't cook," she said.

"You can't?"

"Toast."

"You must cook something."

"Oh, sure. I make great—" she gestured with her free hand. "Reservations. At restaurants."

Emet laughed.

"But you make something out of nothing," she said.

"So what?"

"I've had a lot of nothing in my life," she said. "I'd like to be able to make it into something. But—I can't do that by myself."

Emet's smile flashed in the darkening night. "You stick with me, and I promise I'll always cook for you."

"Deal." Her grin was new-hatched delight.

"Anything else?" he said.

"What do you mean?"

"I mean, I like you because you're sexy and smart and funny."

Mercey blushed.

"So," he went on, "there better be more than you like me because I cook."

A smile lit on her lips and flew away. "You want the list?"

"There's a list?"

"I'm very organized."

Emet turned toward her and put his hand on her knee. “Let’s hear the list.”

Mercey set her hand on his. It was smaller than his, the nails short and neat, no polish. “Emet. I feel good when I’m with you. I like you because no one ever offered to buy me breakfast before unless it was part of a come-on. I like you because even though you never said it, I knew I could run to you when my shit hit the cosmic fan. I like you because you’re not afraid of my brother. And because—” Her voice broke off, and her hand stiffened. Emet shifted his fingers so they were intertwined with hers. Their hands clenched then relaxed, lying loosely knotted together. Mercey held her back straight and her head high, refusing to bow under the pressing ballast of emotion. The darkness seemed to magnify her eyes, which were clear lenses over pools of nightfall. “Because when I’m with you I feel like I can come back from the far side of nowhere.”

Emet put his free hand around her shoulder, and she nested her head against him.

“Sorry,” she said. “Sorry, sorry, sorry.”

“You didn’t make the rules either.”

“My family’s a wreck,” she said “It’s my fault you got sent back in.”

“It’s not your fault, and forget your family,” he said. “It’s a good list. Mostly.”

She lifted her head. "What mostly?"

"The breakfast thing," he said. "How do you know it wasn't part of a come-on?"

She giggled against his sweatshirt.

"I mean, give me some credit here."

"Okay," she said. "You're a conniving letch."

"Now we're cooking with gas." His arm stayed around her. "You want to know something else?" he said to the top of her head. "Truthfully. I am afraid of your brother."

She looked up at him. "Really?"

"I'd be a fool not to be."

"Damn. Another illusion bites the dust."

"But the rest of it sounds about right."

"Okay," she said. She sat up and pulled her purse onto her shoulder. "Want to see my new place? I'm about 97% unpacked."

"What's the other 3%?"

"We may never find out."

They walked through the park side by side. There was a pleasing space between them, full of lights in shadow, as they stepped away together into all things old and new.

THE END

Acknowledgements

The notion that books are created in solitude usually gets a belly laugh out of anyone who has ever written one. With that in mind, I'd like to bring my pit crew out of the shadows into the sunlight of gratitude they so richly deserve.

First and perhaps loudest, I must thank Mike Marano, whose trenchant observations deepened my characters and tightened my prose. To read a manuscript that has gone through the Marano Mill is to have received an MFA via marginalia. (Samples: "Not sure dialogue by proxy works in this context," and "Clay is dumb and messed up.")

I must also thank Karl Colón, good friend and eagle-eyed former prosecutor who explained to me that I'd gotten Clay into a much bigger legal pickle than I'd thought, and no way was he getting off with probation and a stern talking to.

Karen Swank and Kerry Keefe at the Massachusetts Department of Correction supplied me with a level of detail regarding prison life that no second-hand research could have provided. Karen's comments on an early draft of *Second Helpings* steered me around plot holes that were invisible to me until she pointed them out. Many thanks.

My incarcerated students kept me up to snuff with correct use of prison slang, both intentionally and inadvertently.

Chief Richard LeBlond of the MSPCA Law Enforcement Department was courteous, impressively well-informed, and beyond generous when I asked him about the Commonwealth's animal protection laws and procedures. Dr. Flavia Zorgniotti, who has been taking care of my dogs for over a decade, described clinical procedures for a dog in Serena's situation, and let me know in no uncertain terms how she would respond to a case of animal cruelty.

Michelle Kish, PT, DPT, MS, filled me in on the life of a physical therapist, from course load to caseload. Without her input, Mercey would have been far less authentic, and might very well have remained a nurse.

Nicole Blank, store manager at Starbucks (aka "my office"), helped me nail down the various large and small realities of running a neighborhood coffee shop.

Nate and Elwyn, you are the best cheering squad any mom could ever hope for. Thanks for your love and confidence in me. Someday I promise I'll write something you're allowed to read.

Last but never least is Doug Jacobs, my harshest critic and bestest friend. Hearing him read *Second Helpings* aloud was a revelation—I had no idea I was so talented, funny, and insightful. That's probably because without him, I'm not.

Thanks Doug, for everything you do, especially the stuff you think doesn't matter. Love you ridiculously much.

About the Author

Tilia Klebenov Jacobs is a graduate of Oberlin College and Harvard Divinity School. When Tilia is not writing she is teaching (aka "getting paid for bossing people around"). She has taught middle school, high school, and college; currently she teaches writing to prison inmates, and is a judge in the Soul-Making Keats Literary Competition in San Francisco. Her fiction and nonfiction have been published to critical acclaim. Tilia lives near Boston with her husband, two children, and two standard poodles.

Made in the USA
Columbia, SC
01 September 2018